Mystery House Puk

What To Do About POTASS

A comedic novella of political errors

By

Glenn Shepard

www.glennshepardauthor.com

Mystery House Publishing, Inc.

www.mysteryhousepublishing.com

First Edition

ISBN-13: 978-0-9905893-7-2

Cover illustration by Kyra Dunn

Cover design by Ana C. Magno

Printed in The United States of America

Other Books by Glenn Shepard

The Missile Game (Dr. Scott James Thriller #1)

"Slick and intelligent, *The Missile Game* is a thrill ride."
~ Layton Green, author of the Dominic Grey series

"Could be an entire season of 24, it's that fast, that engrossing." ~ *Men Reading Books*

The Zombie Game (Dr. Scott James Thriller #2)

"An action-packed thriller, cleverly plotted, frighteningly imaginative, and shockingly good. *The Zombie Game* will leave you breathless." ~ Martin Jay Weiss, author of *The Alchemist Agenda* and *The Flamingo Coast*

"*The Zombie Game* has it all – twists, turns, and tons of action." ~ Ben Lieberman, author of *Odd Jobs* and *The Carnage Account*

The Ebola Game (Dr. Scott James Thriller #3)

"It's a wild ride that just keeps coming at you."
~ John Haslett, author of *The Lost Raft*

The Encryption Game (Dr. Scott James Thriller #4)

"*The Encryption Game* is another non-stop thrill ride from a master thriller writer. You can read it on its own or as the fourth addition to one of the best thriller series out there right now. It's a high-altitude balloon flight that leaves you gasping for breath. It's a must read for any thriller fan. Enjoy and have a defibrillator close by because this one will stop your heart!"
~ Richard Krevolin, author of *Screenwriting in the Land of Oz* and *Screenwriting from the Soul*

This tale satirizes the ineptness of fictional legislators, of the same and opposing political parties, when they react as adversaries of a fictional, sometimes-dysfunctional, executive branch of government.

This story is a parody and a satire and a work of friction and fiction. Any resemblance to any true events or presidents or political figures is purely coincidental, and any ill will toward any real life personages is highly deplorable and not the intent of the author or the story.

In fact, if you think you have found any apparent or hidden meaning in this work, the author will disavow it. And yes, at times it may contain vulgar language because, well, it's about politics. In the end, this little novella of political error's only intent is to evoke laughter and maybe make you question our world today and think a little.

And isn't that a good thing for us all to do now and then?

Chapter 1

9 am. The Rosy Bottom Golf Course, Sweetfellow, Florida

The President stepped to the tee box wearing a starched, pressed, white, linen, tailor-fitted golf shirt that fell loosely over his full waist and loose, custom, white trousers with cuffs. His white cap was emblazoned with the bold, red logo, POTASS, under which were small-lettered words, Power Of The American Superior Sovereign. Placing his ball on his tee, he stood tall over the others in his group, with his silver hair and wrinkle-free face glistening in the morning sun.

He observed a party of three elderly golfers still putting on the par three, eighteenth hole one hundred eighty yards ahead of him. He frowned and leaned toward a golf cart parked obscurely in the woods, giving it the "thumbs down" gesture. The cart immediately roared away, crashing through a carefully manicured rose and hyacinth garden, knocking down two newly planted magnolia trees, and sped to the eighteenth hole. Jumping from the cart were three men and one woman, all trim, six feet tall, black-suited, and grim-faced, with crew cuts and wearing sunglasses. They confronted the two elderly men and a woman. After a brief exchange of words, these Secret Service officers threw the two old guys on the ground and were attempting to snap on handcuffs when the woman began swatting at them with her putter. Up drove a second cart ordered by The President, overloaded with five more Men In Black who bounced out and threw the old woman to the ground, muffling her screams with a fist full of handkerchiefs. The President ignored the commotion and continued to play.

The newly appointed secretary of state, Michael Emerson, saw immediately that the multitude of black suits and old golfers were in danger of being KO-ed by The President's ball. Despite his hunched forward posture and bowed legs, Emerson jumped up and down, shouting "Fore! Fore!" The barely five-foot, six-inch tall appointee then saw the ball slice. The green cap with the logo, Rosy Bottom Golf, fell from his head, exposing his red, splotched, bald pate with a puff of brown hair over each ear. He stood momentarily to tuck in his electric-purple shirttail that hung over his paunch, then jumped up and down again. With his right arm held straight out to alert the group ahead that the ball was flying to the right of the hole, he again shouted, "Fore! Fore!"

The President was placing his nine iron in his bag as his low-flying ball landed in the back of a sand trap well away from the green.

Chief of Staff Joe Smith stood with his left leg crossed over his right, showing off his yellow with black squares, thin-waisted, leg-hugging Bonobos. He leaned on his pitching wedge as he waited for the group ahead to do The President's bidding, rope the old men and woman and, like hunters, lash them to the front of their carts. He wore his bright green ivy cap high on his forehead, showing off his square jaw, rugged cheekbones, and unnaturally black hair for a man of sixty.

The leader of the Secret Service shouted to The President as their carts drove away, "Two bucks and a doe!"

The President raised his thumb, then turned to Smith. "Go on, go on! We don't have all day."

Smith placed his ball on the tee and stroked the ball smoothly. The high-arching ball came to rest within a foot of the hole.

Emerson swung as hard as he could with his three iron and sent a low-trajectory ball bouncing along the fairway from thirty feet away to the fringes of the green.

The fourth member of the party, seventy-eight-year-old Labor Secretary Hardy Workman, watched with a rigid, poker-stiff back. He wore conservative, solid black Nike shirt and trousers. His furrowed face with heavy jowls and hanging neck folds was dotted with age spots. With a score already well over 100, he pocketed his ball.

The President jumped in his jazzed-up golf cart with the gold-plated monograms dotted all over it and a custom-made license plate, all marked with only six letters, POTASS. With oversized wheels and a souped-up engine on a 650-amp controller, he roared away at thirty miles an hour. Three golf carts loaded with black-suited Secret Service men and women followed closely.

Emerson, Smith, and Workman crowded into a Rosy Bottom Club cart and followed well behind. The

President was already at the hole with his putter as they parked. Emerson walked to the sand trap and pointed. "There's your ball, Mr. President."

"No. That ball is marked, 'POTASS 3'. It's Workman's ball. Mine is a . . ." He fumbled in his pocket, pulled out a ball, and looked at it. "Mine's a 'POTASS 2'." He walked to the hole with his back to the others and, with the "POTASS 2" still in his hand, reached in the hole. "Look. A hole in one! That's fantastic. No other president has ever done that! And my score for the match will be under seventy! Eisenhower will turn in his grave."

Smith and Workman clapped their hands. "Great shot, and a fantastic round of golf!" they said, as Emerson retrieved the "POTASS 3" ball and handed it to Workman.

In a private room in the clubhouse, they were served their beverages; scotch and waters for Smith and Workman, a Virgin Mary for Emerson, and a Diet Coke for The President.

The President turned to his recently appointed secretary of state. "Mr. Emerson, what are your ideas about foreign policy?"

Emerson's lips twitched as he began to laugh. "You mean 'Fore-In'? Like our golf today, I yell 'Fore'! and you say, 'In the hole.' Get it? That's your 'Fore-in' policy." He began an intensifying laughter.

The others looked solemnly at him.

" 'Fore-in' policy. Don't you guys get it?"

After turning his back on the jokester for a few seconds, The President abruptly twisted, revealing a sour face. "Give me one of your specifics about," he paused a moment before spelling out, "F . . . O . . . R . . . A . . . I . . . N . . . policy."

Emerson cleared his throat with an "A-hem" and said quietly, "You are wrong to be so hard on the Chinese. With all their investments in America, they own a considerable part of The United States already. They are our largest business partner. And their trade agreements are a big reason for our current economic success. We . . . you . . . should drop these horrific tariffs on imported goods from their country."

The President stood and gestured to two Secret Service officers standing outside the door. They brought brushes to wipe lint from his golf shirt. As a Secret

Service man opened the door for him to leave, he looked to the wall behind Emerson's head as he said, "Emerson, you're fired. I don't like your foreign policy and you're dressed like a circus clown. You act like one too. Look at Smith. He's outfitted like I expect of a man in a prominent White House office."

Smith smiled as he stood at attention with his drink in his hand.

The President next addressed Smith. "You'll have to improve your game before we play again. You're fired too. Use the free time to brush up on your game."

Smith's drink slipped, crashing to the floor, without movement of any part of his hand or body.

"Workman, you played a masterful game of golf. I enjoyed having you in my foursome. I'll see you back at Capitol Hill."

As the door was closing behind the departing president, Emerson stormed from the clubhouse. When passing The President's golf cart, he stopped and kicked the tires repeatedly. With his hands making the shape of a megaphone around his mouth, he yelled at the top of his voice, "This cart should be labelled PŎT-ĂSS, not PŌ-

TAHSS! He's not the Power Of The American Superior Sovereign. He's the Power Of The Asshole Sovereign Supreme! He's POTASSHOLE!"

Two policemen promptly came and led him away, kicking and screaming, "POTASSHOLE! POTASSHOLE! POTASSHOLE!"

<u>Chapter 2</u>

10:45 am the same day.
The Cabinet Room in the White House

The President sat in his chair in the West Wing conducting the first meeting of his cabinet in the past two months. He looked around at the group he had appointed and the two empty seats of men whom he'd fired after golf this morning, then announced, "Today, the meeting will be brief." He looked at his watch. "I have a firm commitment at eleven."

The man to his left, Secretary of Defense Danny Dapper, said quickly, "But I have a number of issues to discuss with you."

Several others spoke up at the same time, interrupting each other, with Transportation Secretary Harry Johns saying, "The flight controllers are about to strike, and we need to hire . . ."

Chief of Homeland Security Skip Church stated, "I must tell you about a new high school shooting in

Illinois. You have to take time to listen to my recommendations as the best way to prevent more . . ."

Health and Human Services Secretary Bab Babs Callins stood and, with her squeaky voice, spoke as loudly as she could to be heard over all the others. "The measles epidemic is rampant. Can you do one of your Executive Orders to force inoculations of . . ."

She was interrupted by five others, all talking over each other, who demanded — no, begged is a better word in this situation in the White House — to have their needs discussed with The President.

The President held both hands out to quiet the group around the table but still had to speak over the other voices: "Listen, just listen. This is important. Tina Tarantula has a special report on FAXY News. I have to listen. She's speaking on my criticism of Puerto Rico and their misuse of all the aid money I gave them. She's the only other genius person in the world. She agrees with my position. I must see that, and all of you should do so yourselves. Now, Secretary Dapper, what do you have to report?"

"I have five issues."

"I'll take the top two."

Dapper said quickly, "The Chinese. They're claiming the Sparsely Islands, which are in international waters. They're setting up missile bases there and . . ."

"Oh, yes. Set me up with a face-to-face meeting with the Chinese leader day after tomorrow, here in the White House. He's a fine individual. A good person, and I respect him highly. He and I are good friends, and we really like each other."

The acting commerce secretary spoke quickly, "But on the day after tomorrow you've invited the President of France and our national dodge ball champions. We can't possibly add another dignitary."

"Then cancel the President of France. Now Secretary Dapper, give me your second topic."

"The NATO Alliance needs direction as to whether they have our support if Russia continues to advance troops beyond Crimea."

"Connect me with them in about a month after I meet Russia's Foreign Minister, Snegari Kolcockitch. He and I are good friends and I'll ask his advice on that one.

I'll take one last report. Secretary Chickenpooper, do you have a report on the Fourth of July extravaganza?"

Interior Secretary Clayton Higgenlooper's face turned scarlet red as he took a deep breath and tried to quiet his racing pulse. Higgenlooper, a retired Army general, was dressed in his formal, Army Blue dress uniform with multitudes of gold and silver bars and colorful decorations that spilled well below his thin waist and onto the sides of his coat. He sat with a stiff posture that accented his six-two, muscular frame. "Mr. President, sir. The tanks you ordered for the Fourth of July parade, sir, pose intrinsic difficulties, sir. There are several problems, sir. The engineering it will take to move them from Ft. Sewer to the Lincoln Memorial, sir, makes it, sir, an impossible undertaking, sir."

"But General Chickenpooper . . ."

"Sir. That's Higgenlooper, sir."

"Yes, yes. You had no problem getting your tanks from Ft. Sewer to Iraq. Just do it."

"Sir. Yes, sir."

"And last night I had brilliant idea. I have great admiration for the Chinese, and every year they have the greatest parade in the world that displays all their military hardware. I want this year's Fourth of July parade to be as grand. Move one of my new Virginia Class subs to the Lincoln Memorial. Place it right in front of the celebrity grandstand I ordered built."

"Sir. The Chinese have only four modern submarines, and Intelligence tells me that none of them are functional at this time, sir."

"If the Chinese had a sub that was functional, you could bet your bippy they'd have one in their parade."

"But Mr. President, sir. To move a 7,300-ton sub, sir, from the water, sir, to the Lincoln Memorial, sir, is an impossible task, sir."

"But Chickenpooper . . ."

"Sir, that's Higgenlooper, sir."

"Chickenpooper, The Lincoln Memorial is right on the Potomac River, with the reflective pond at its back, is it not?"

"Sir. Yes, sir."

"Then motor the boat . . ."

"Sir, that's a ship, not a boat, sir."

"Then just pull it to the shore and have a crane hoist it either to the parade route, or place it in the reflective pool."

General Higgenlooper's left eye began to twitch. "Sir. It will be easier, sir, to move the Lincoln Memorial than the submarine, sir."

The President scratched his chin. "That's a good idea. I hadn't thought of that. Research my idea of moving the Lincoln Memorial, Chickenpooper."

The twitch in Higgenlooper's eye spread to his arms and shoulders. He folded his arms around his chest to stop his shaking and then began to laugh hysterically as he snatched the bars and ribbons from his coat and threw them at other cabinet members. "Heh, heh, heh. Did you see that, sir, Mr. President, sir? My Silver Star landed in Squeaky Callins' hair. Here, I'll try to put a Legion of Merit in Danny Dapper's pocket."

The President snapped his fingers, and two Secret Service officers dragged General Higgenlooper from the Cabinet Room. "Shut him up and get him out of here," The President ordered.

The general wrestled away from the guards and vibrated his straight index finger up and down between his lips, creating the oscillating bleat of a birthing ewe: "Heh . . . heh . . . he, he, he, he, he, he, heheh."

An officer duct-taped his mouth shut.

The President pounded the desk with his fist and stood to leave. "Meeting dismissed."

Johns, Dapper, Callins, and Church exited slowly. As they approached the door together, Dapper whispered the code words, "Operation Ten Little Indians a go."

The other three nodded affirmatively.

Chapter 3

10 pm the same day. The women's basement bathroom in the US Capitol Building

"Heart attack," a quiet voice by the door penetrated the darkness.

"You can't do heart attacks," came a barely audible, muffled voice that echoed just slightly off the tile walls of a small, completely dark bathroom.

"Why do you say that, Harry, uh, Squirrel?"

Loud *Shhh*'s came from three others.

Callins' squeaky voice whispered, "You know better than to use names, Danny."

"You forgot already! My code is Rabbit," Dapper stated.

More *Shhh*'s came, including from Harry Johns, whose muffled voice followed. "The drugs that cause heart failure are traceable because we'd need a doctor or druggist to supply it, and those groups can't keep their mouths closed. We'll all go to jail if The President learns what we're up to. By the way, do any of our colleagues know of our meeting and what we're discussing?"

"No."

"No."

Callins spoke. "I'm afraid to talk about it with anyone else. Surely others feel the way we do, but if I even discuss it with them, it could backfire on us. We've all waited for others to attempt something to shut this president up, but nobody other than us, his own cabinet members . . ."

"Shh! There are ears everywhere, Cow."

"But I don't want to be coded a cow. Call me Cat."

"Ok, you're Cat."

"Thanks, I like Cat," Callins said, before continuing. "We have no means of effective communication with The President. Like today. We had a fifteen-minute session, accomplished nothing, and then, *Bam!* — the meeting concludes. He doesn't listen to our concerns and makes erratic decisions on his own, tweeting his directives in the middle of the night when we're trying to sleep. We don't know what he's thinking until we read about it the next day. He's putting the safety of the entire country in jeopardy. We're obligated to our nation to do something about the situation."

"If he stays in power, we'll all be as looney as General Pigeongooper."

"That's Higgenlooper."

"Oh."

"Agreed. And let's keep it quiet," Harry said, with a stern tone to his voice.

A subtle bathroom odor spiraled lightly, up and over the bathroom stall, settling gently in the room.

Skip Church waved the air in front of his nose and said, in a coarse, gravelly voice, "I know your knees are so bad you have to sit, but that's just crude."

A muffled voice replied from the other side of the stall. "This is a bathroom."

The squeaky voice stated, "And it is a lady's room."

"Then I yield to the lady cabinet secretary from Maine. Your turn is next."

"Harry, uh, Squirrel…"

"Shh!"

"At least open the door to the stall so we can hear you."

Harry leaned forward on the toilet seat, released the door latch, and shoved it open.

Whack!

Church grabbed his nose and grunted. "You broke my nose!"

The three *Shhh* birds returned.

"It's bleeding! Get me some paper towels!"

"Hold your horses," came the squeaky voice, as she felt her way between two men, tiptoed through the darkness, and lightly slipped three paper towels from the dispenser to Skip Church, the man with the bloody nose. As she passed them to her injured friend, she said, "My vote is for your California 17 ½ Street Gang; you know, the Mexicans. Our CIA briefed us about the three ex-Army snipers that work through that group. They made political "erasures" from over a thousand yards in Lebanon and Myanmar. They had CIA help to escape, but here in the US, they'll just sneak over to Mexico and never be caught."

"But shooting somebody? That's criminal, and murder's a serious crime."

"If we Republicans don't somehow stop The President's callous administration by Twitter . . ."

"We've all tried, but he just doesn't listen to anybody. He decides on things and bypasses all the rest of us . . ."

"He's a loose cannon, and none of us are going to change that."

"There are a lot of voters out there who are following his erratic actions. Anybody that reads a newspaper can see what he's doing to our country, and CNS reporters openly state the lies he tells and of blunders he's making in foreign policy."

"As bad as it sounds, he must be removed from office or the Democrats will easily win the next election."

"Then I'll be out of a job. In fact, we'd all be out."

"You can run for the Senate again."

From the gravelly voice came, "But none of us will get elected again, and I haven't worked for twenty-five years, since first voted in to Congress. And, I don't want to work again. In fact, I don't know how to work after doing government stuff for so long. But I have to get a salary to pay expenses and all, like we get with our government entitlements."

"And fork dough out of our own pockets for travels to Maui or St. Barts."

"True, Blowfish . . ."

"No. You're Blowfish. I'm Rabbit."

"Oh. Rabbit, I'm just saying, I couldn't take my two-week vacation every year in Scotland if I didn't claim it to be 'government-related'."

Callins spoke. "I agree with you all. I'd only get $139,200 a year in my retirement package. And that's not enough to pay for my lifestyle. I'd go bankrupt."

Dapper said quietly, "Me too. So, to keep what we have, The President must go. Vice President Pennypincher is such a nice guy. If we can just have him step in and be president, we can feel proud we've done our jobs to maintain the Democracy as spelled out by the Constitution."

Church, in a coarse tone, said, "The bonus is that we'll all keep our jobs and our Republican friends will get re-elected. Then we wouldn't have to get a real job and be poor again."

"What if The President gets impeached and the vice president gets the job?"

"Republicans would have their jobs only until the next election. Then the impeachment will ensure the Democrats will be elected for not only The President and vice president, but all Senate and House seats."

"You sure about that?"

"Yeah. Tiger Schweitzer says that all the time on CNS, and all the political experts tell the same story as well."

From the gravelly voice came, "Yeah. He says that so often, it must be so."

"I like Stevey Coldbear."

"But he's a comedian, not a political expert."

"What does he say?"

"Oh, just stuff about The President. Sometimes he's funny. Oh, and he also talks with celebrities and politicians. Oh, yeah, and he has a great band and . . ."

"I like Jimmy Felon. He cracks me up with his musical contests and how he can't stop laughing."

Harry grunted, then asked, "Can we please get back on track? We're here at this hour for a reason. If we don't do something about this president, what's going to happen to America?"

"For one thing, the women's soccer team, the Bean Town Patriarchs and Brute teams, as well as John John Stew-Wart, "Hanky" Hankers, LeBonbon Jims, Mack Curly, K.K. Do-Rant and Lowe Kappersnapper will never get to go to the White House."

"So? They all have money enough to buy the White House and not invite Mr. President to come see them. Turnabout is fair play."

"The President would insist he has more dough than all of them, but if he bought it, he'd fill in the reflective pool and and make a golf course in the shadow of the Washington Monument."

After a pause of less than half a minute, Church said quietly, "As much as he hates Mexicans, the 17 ½ Street Gang is perfect to do the job."

"How do you know about the 17 ½ Street guys?"

"I was raised on 16th Street. We played cowboys and Indians together. They used real bullets."

Harry spoke from the commode. "No doubt they could do it, but their CIA contacts were quiet after the foreign eradications. The CIA will be very vocal when a President of the United States is 'neutralized'. There's no way of protecting them in this situation."

"So, what's the down side of that? With that gang all gone?"

"I'd miss my childhood buddies."

"But with their 1000-yard range with the US sniper rifles, they can do it. There are lots of days when he's in the open at that distance."

The woman replied, "He'd be a sitting duck to the Mexican snipers."

"I'm on record as opposing the shooting of waterfowl," Church said.

Dapper replied, "Be quiet on that issue. Half your electorate are hunters."

The now-quiet voice near the door said, "I actually don't like blood. And don't say 'sitting ducks'. I like ducks as much as my electorate."

"But those duck hunters are so nutsy about their sport. Put a Donald Duck cap on The President's head, one with the bill that looks like a duck's, and say that he's a last of the Giant Squawk Duck endangered species. They'd stand in line to fill him full of buckshot," were the words of Johns.

Callins spoke, "Blood is awfully messy. I don't like to look at it, let alone touch it.

"You won't have to touch it."

"But we'll be right with him when it goes down, and we'll have to pretend to resuscitate him. Yuck."

Dapper continued, "I assure you, there's no blood with a heart attack."

"There's not?"

"More importantly, a heart attack isn't likely to create an investigation, particularly since modern medicine has developed deadly drugs that are undetectable. The death certificate would read, 'Death by Natural Causes-Coronary Insufficiency'. There'd be no query to expose our cover. That gets my vote."

"What about a hair dryer in his bathtub?" Church asked.

Callins' voice again penetrated the darkness. "I know several of his lady valets who think he's a sexist pig. They'd take pleasure in doing the hair dryer thing. Let's give that consideration."

"Yes. Why don't you look into it?"

Harry said from his seat, "Now, I like that. Let's investigate the hair dryer. Who's in favor?"

After a pause, Church said, "Me."

There was quiet for half a minute before Callins nodded her head and said, "I can go for that."

The three turned to Dapper, the quiet proponent of the heart attack method. "And are you with us, Rabbit?"

"Not me."

Harry shifted his weight on the commode seat as he spoke gruffly. "But there are three 'yesses', and our vote will prevail in this democratic ruling. Now I have to be in a committee hearing in a few minutes. Meeting dismissed."

The heart attack proponent held his ground as the woman tried to push him away from the door. "Whoa, whoa. Don't any of you want my minority opinion?"

Harry said, with his voice raised in anger, "Talk about heart attacks another day."

Dapper responded, "How did I ever hook up with you three? You're all a bunch of ding-dongs. You know, The President said once at a cabinet meeting that he took a shower that morning. It was on one of the days when he told everyone how great everything's going, when it's not ever so great. Doesn't that change our strategy?"

Callins chimed in. "Yes, you're right. And I heard on a late-night comedy show that The President likes golden showers in his gold-plated bathrooms."

"That's different. Don't go there."

"So? What's different? I like the color match gold fixtures and a gold shower. Sounds pretty."

"Ask that question to one of your daughters, but don't say 'golden showers' to anyone else. You'll embarrass yourself."

"Huh?"

The gruff voice interrupted, "Well, have one of the valets throw the hair dryer in the shower."

"Whoooa. It may give him a hot foot, but don't expect anything more. Let's look at heart attacks."

The toilet seat squeaked as the sitting man rose. "OK. I gotta go. Look at heart attack drugs. But I prefer the sniper. Serves The President right, as much as he hates the Mexicans. There's a lot of 'em who'd want to pull the trigger."

"But I like the hair dryer."

"And we haven't talked about poisons."

"Geez. We're about as decisive as Congress."

Dapper moved to open the door but in his abrupt turn squarely smacked Skip Church's bleeding nose with his shoulder. The wounded man screamed as the others, showing no compassion, filtered into the dimly lit basement hallway of the Capitol Building.

A janitor who was napping on the floor of this isolated area was awakened by the *bump* and scream, raised one eye open to witness the three men and one woman leaving the tiny basement woman's bathroom, put there for the employees. "These lawmakers are one crazy group," he whispered and closed his eye in sleep. The next morning, he reported the unusual occurrence to his friend, Maintenance Supervisor Thomas Wilson.

Wilson replied, "That's interesting. Thanks for telling me. I'll put that under my hat for now and suggest you do the same."

Chapter 4

5:30 pm a week later. A bench beside a newsstand outside the Capitol Building

Thomas Wilson sat reading a *Washington Unposted* newspaper he "borrowed" from the newsstand beside him, when his frequent companion, Cabinet Member Hollie Mackril, came along, shaking a bag in the air. "I brought the Cokes. Do you have the snacks?"

Mackril was an attractive fifty-year-old woman with straight, brown, shoulder-length hair that nicely curled up at the shoulder line. She sat beside him. Wilson lifted his five-eleven, trim, fit body to a half stand and bowed slightly. He ran his hand over his thick, two-inch-long, brown hair that was tapered on the sides and, as always, neatly combed. "What a pleasure it is to see you again, Ms. Mackril, and yes, I have our usual; peanut butter and jelly sandwiches." He pointed to his small, fold-up cooler.

"I'm hungry," she said, as she unzipped the cooler and took her sandwich.

She took a bite before saying, "It's a pleasure to still be here, with all the shake-ups in the White House." Then she laughed and added, "I may be next, but I'll go down fighting."

"Like a fish out of water, as you said on your last visit to this bench."

Hollie Mackril from Wisconsin was The President's current secretary of housing and re-development, but cabinet positions seemed to be coming and going on almost a week by week interval.

Since Wilson took the job of maintenance supervisor at the Capitol Building, she visited him regularly on Wednesdays after her conference with the Senate majority leader. She had been a friend of Senator Fargo, who'd originally employed Wilson as his handyman. Wilson was an exceptionally hard worker and bright, even though he'd dropped out of school at age fourteen to work and support his mother and six siblings. Mackril had been instrumental in helping him gain his job as maintenance supervisor in the Capitol Building when Fargo retired and joined his former law partnership goup, Martin, Lartin, Barten, and Fargo.

"I wanted to ask your opinion about my Housing For The Poor program I'm pushing," Mackril said.

Wilson was an avid reader and spent time on this park bench every day reading newspapers and journals. This, combined with his contact with others in his socio-economic strata, made him a target for members of the Cabinet, House, and Senate alike, who consistently sought his opinion as to the needs and perspectives of his people. His honest replies superseded, to her, the opinions of all the popular Washington pundits.

As they talked, Mackril noticed the presidential limousine drive up and park a block away. She stood abruptly, saying, "One of us is being scrutinized by The President himself."

Wilson looked up to see the man in the back seat of the limousine lean out the window, watching them through binoculars. Mackril stood and quickly walked away, saying, "Only one of us is in trouble, but both of us will be fired." She didn't laugh.

The limo motored slowly to the park bench and stopped. A chauffer bounded from the car and opened the back door. The President stepped out and was lifting the binocular strap from around his neck when his hand twisted in the cord. The driver reached to assist, but the growling President pushed the cord, which was still hanging from his neck, over the driver's hand. The driver's hand became entangled in the cord, which was still wrapped around The President's hand while still hanging from his neck. "Do something!" he screamed.

The limo guy put his other hand (the last hand he had left) into the maze of hands, cords, and The President's neck. The President yanked the cord, trying to free himself from the mess, throwing the driver on the back seat. The man's legs went up in the air with the tumble, twisting yet another appendage in the conglomeration of body parts engulfed in the binocular's cord. The President fell, face down, on top of his driver.

Wilson knew he had to do something to help and jumped into the position of attempted savior to an awkward presidential situation. As he raised a pocket knife to cut the binocular strap, The President lifted his other arm to shield his face. In so doing, it, too, became entangled with the binocular strap.

From a second government, black Chevy Suburban, a man jumped out. His fist landed squarely on Wilson's right eye, knocking him to the sidewalk. He twisted the knife from Wilson's hand, threw him to the pavement, and encircled him in a bear hold. A four-man team rushed to The President, untangled the binoculars, and brushed his black suit.

The President said, "I'll take the knife. I have a grandson who'd like it. And let the man go. He's with me."

He was breathing heavily as he led Wilson to the park bench and sat. "Will Thompson. Can I call you that?"

"Um . . . Well . . . Ah . . . Yes. Yes, sir."

"I hear you are quite a student of politics."

"I . . . I didn't go to college, but . . ."

"I know all about your past, and there's no need for any apology."

"Then know also that I uh, uh am impressed by g . . . g . . . good things you've done as President."

The President shook his head in approval. "Yes, and I agree with you. I have done so many great things that far exceed all the prior presidents put together."

Wilson's head dropped as a sign of respect, and he wiped the blood from his right eye.

"A bad black eye you have. Stop playing Frisbee and put a filet mignon on your big bruise. It takes the swelling out."

"Uh, thanks?"

"Yes. You are wise, despite your many deficiencies."

"M . . . My deficiencies?"

"Yes. By the time I was your age, I had banked a hundred million dollars. You are still short of your first million."

Wilson raised his eyebrows as his shoulders danced back and forth. "Sure. About n . . . nine hundred and ninety-nine thousand, nine hundred and ninety-nine dollars. That's, uh, a little short I'd say."

The President shook his head slightly back and forth. "My sympathies. Poverty is a character flaw. You must work harder to correct that."

Wilson leaned back on the bench. "Huh?"

"Yes. Just watch what I do."

"B . . . b . . . but, you . . . you . . . you're President. You don't have time to spend manipulating money transactions."

"But if you handle money well, as I always do, being The President is simple. As I always say, if you know money, you know people. And you've witnessed how well I run the country. That's because I know money. When I speak, people stop and listen . . ."

"Just like E.F. Hutton?"

"Hutton? Who's he? Has this E.F. Hutton tried to steal my byword?"

"Uhh . . ."

"So. Already you see all the respect I have and how easily I get things done."

"R . . . r . . . really?"

The President turned and looked into Wilson's eyes. "Several of my Republican friends have conversed with you and they tell me of the broad scope of knowledge you've shared with them. It's good for you, one of my loyal supporters, to have your unbiased opinions of my perfect policies. It's important for me to have your reliable approval and always worshipful admonition . . ."

Wilson interrupted him "You mean ad . . . ad . . . admiration, not admonition. Admonition means a warning or an administrative rebuke. You don't mean th . . . th . . . that."

"Yes, didn't I say that? Will Thompson, you must pay more attention to my words. My diction is perfect, and I abhor your correcting my language, with your speech as poor as it is. And as I was saying, together we must show the other side of the 'false news' they print about me all the time. Come to my office tomorrow. I'd like to have your input on some perplexing issues." He stood to leave, adding quickly, "And also, Will Thompson, since you are such a loyal fan of mine, I have a job for you."

He stepped in the open door of his limo as a black-suited man bounced from the front seat and handed Wilson an envelope with his name on it. "Give this to the attendant at the White House Northwest Gate promptly at

5:30 am. That will gain your entrance. And The President says, 'Don't forget to put steak fillets on the eye.' "

Chapter 5

5:30 am the next morning. The White House

As Wilson was ushered by a guard toward the Oval Office, they encountered a woman running in the hall away from that office, tucking in her blouse and dragging her purse by its broken strap.

"Morning, Miss Brantly," Wilson's usher said.

The woman kept her head down and didn't reply.

A red, laced bra lay in the partially open door to the Oval Office. The attendant lifted it and placed it out of sight behind his back as he escorted Wilson to The President.

Wilson had been made mentally and emotionally strong by his early conversion from a growing teenager to man of the household in the role of breadwinner, as well as a shoulder for his mother to cry on. The job had been too great for his dad, who had deserted them and moved to California, even with Thomas and six other kids, one a newborn and all the rest under ten years. Wilson was determined to be strong and fill the void. Because of that, however, he had a weakness: he was intimidated by, and would become flustered around, individuals in top leadership positions, especially when he first met them. Because of that, he was trembling as he faced The Man, with his eye still swollen so badly he could barely see from it.

The President, sitting at his desk, studied Wilson for a couple minutes, with his elbows on the desk and his chin resting on his clasped hands. Wilson's fear was obvious.

The President's first words were, "Will Thompson, you have a black eye. How many times do I have to tell you to stay away from those playing Frisbee on the Capitol lawn?"

"Uh, uh . . ." Wilson stuttered, as he tried to think of a reply.

"Do you like my Resolute desk? It was a gift from Queen Victoria to Rutherford Hayes in 1804."

Wilson stopped for a second but quickly made the correction. "Yes, sir. Uh, our country located the HMS *Resolute* after it was iced in and abandoned by British Arctic explorers. Uh, they repaired the ship and returned it to the B . . . British in 1856 as a peace gesture. Over, uh, twenty years later, after the two countries had been through a f . . . few more escalating tensions, like the conflict in the Pig War in the San Juan islands, Q . . . Queen Victoria returned the favor in 1880 b . . . by making this beautiful desk from timbers of the ship after it was, uh, uh, dismantled."

The President tilted his head back and pursed his lips.

In the long and painful two minutes Wilson waited for a reaction, he conjured up ideas that his remarks were interpreted as offensive. He felt a great relief as The President nodded approval. "Yes, yes." But his anguish returned when The President asked, "That's how we acquired Puerto Rico, isn't it?"

Sweat moistened Wilson's brow as he thought for an escape from a brazen response to The President's error. "Uh, w . . . well, it was the Oregon Territory and the San Juan Islands in the uh, Pacific Northwest that we f . . . fought for and were successful in our stand-off against Great Britain. Then, uh, y . . . yes, that was another of our country's subtle wars with a European country that few . . . other . . . people recall, so I, uh, I applaud your perception of even the most minute historical details."

The President, now smiling broadly, leaned forward in his chair and asked, "The Pig War. What's that all about?"

Wilson responded quickly. "Uh, a British pig wandered into land the American military claimed as part of the Oregon Territory. A f . . . farmer shot the pig. And that, uh, inflamed the hostility."

The President laughed. "Yes, I knew that. Pigs. It's funny. I was just testing you." He studied an uncomfortable Wilson up and down for what seemed a long time before resuming the conversation.

"Will Thompson, I know you read a lot and that you comprehend what you read. I thought of hiring a number of others for the job I'm giving you, but somehow, you seem more sincere than the others in all you do. This work is critical to My Presidency, and that's why I chose you."

Wilson gave a slight smile, reacting to the compliment in no other manner.

"It's important to me, Will Thompson . . ."

His shaking began as he tried to correct the wrong name with which The President addressed him. “Uh, sir, m . . . m . . . my real n . . . n . . . name is T. . . Thomas Wilson.”

“Yes, yes, I know. That’s right. And as I was saying, Will Thompson, I know what's being printed about me in newspapers and news magazines. My White House staff collects all the articles written in English which have anything to do with my job as President. I want you to come to my office every day when you leave the Capitol Building.” He reached into a drawer of the fancy wood-carved desk and removed a foot-long pair of scissors and a postal scale. The President thrust the oversized scissors toward Wilson.

As a surprised Wilson jumped back to avoid being stabbed, his hand fell on a four-inch, red button on the corner of the desk. With his contact, the button lit up, red, bright, and blinking.

Wilson’s arms stiffened at his side as his mouth dropped open. “Yikes!”

"What's wrong, Will Thompson? Are you afraid you've just launched an atomic bomb?" He laughed for a second time.

The color returned to Wilson's face as he straightened his knees and the posture slump created by the event. "Uh . . . uh, no, sir. I feared a trap door would open and I'd fall to a pool of sh . . . sharks below."

"You must be a James Bond fan. In *Thunder Ball*, Bond's nemesis, Blowfield, hit a red button to open up a trap door to a shark pit . . ."

Wilson's face lit up as he said, "I'm a James, uh, Bond fan as well. I've watched all of his films at night on TV since I was a kid. And so, I'm sorry to, uh, contradict you, sir, but the movie was *The Spy Who Loved Me*, and his enemy in that film was actually Karl Stromberg."

The President raised his chin and looked down at Wilson. "Yes, yes, whatever. And what about the red button in that *Dr. Strangelove* movie? The one that launched an atom bomb?"

Wilson recalled that the 1964 movie was a black and white film, with not a touch of red in it, but he didn't push his luck any further. Instead, he shrugged his shoulders and smiled. "Yes, uh, that was a great movie, but what's your impressive red button here for?"

Wilson's question was answered as a young man, wearing black trousers and bow tie with a white tuxedo shirt, entered carrying a can of Diet Coke on a silver tray. The attendant placed the Coke on the desk, then turned to look at Wilson as he slipped a box of animal crackers in an open drawer of the fancy desk. The President closed the drawer rapidly.

"I like Diet Cokes." The President pointed to the button. "This guy brings a Diet Coke each time I press it, at least eighteen times a day. Diet Coke stimulates my whole body and my brain as well. It improves my performance, which I need to stay on top of everything I do. I drink one before my every tweet. In fact, during my most productive days, when I do two dozen tweets in an evening, I just about pop from the heavy intake." He laughed.

"Don't uh, you like beer?"

"I don't drink any form of alcohol. Beer, wine, champagne, or hard liquor? That stuff just eats away at your body and dulls brain function. Number one, alcoholic products are not healthy, and number two, it interferes with my thought processes. I made billions in my business enterprises, and I give the Diet Coke a bit of credit for my well-formulated policy declarations." He puffed his chest out and increased the volume of his voice. "I've made far more money than anyone who's ever lived." His voice quieted. "And in order to stay ahead of my competitors, I must keep my mind free of alcohol's stimulating and depressive actions. I am always the best at everything I do. And I am the best president this nation has ever had, despite unfair criticism from the Democrats, the newspapers, CNS and, now, even FAXY. FAXY, with Billy O'Rilehoo used to be on my team, but not anymore. They're now at the top of my hate list, and I'll get even with them." His hand slipped into the drawer, and he fumbled a moment before grabbing a handful of crackers, popping them into his mouth. I hope you're better than the jerkface that preceded you in this job."

"Huh?"

"He didn't know sausage from Shinola."

"That's shit, uh, sir."

"Yes, that's what I said. Now pay attention."

"Yes, sir."

The President looked down at a fallen cracker in the shape of an elephant. “Elephants are my favorite,” he said, as he put it in his mouth. “This sausage guy only lasted four hours. That was two days ago.”

“So, you’ve been a couple days without help?”

“No, the last one left an hour ago.”

“So, two others held the job in the past two days?

“No. There were five in all. Totally incompetent, the whole batch of them.”

Wilson tried to stop his trembling as he raised his eyebrows and tilted his head before failing at his attempt to smile. “Yes, Mr. President. I'm, uh, on your team. I'll do everything I can to assist you, until I get f . . . fired.”

“My team. I like that. And I’m happy you're a part of it. The President smiled broadly as he picked up the scissors. Your job each day is to cut out every article that mentions my name from all the magazines and newspapers.”

Wilson initially twisted his mouth a little before giving a slight nod of approval.

“Cut each one the same way, Will Thompson.” The President was painfully slow as he demonstrated using a *News Every Other Day* magazine with his photo on front. He meticulously cut off the front cover, slowly keeping the scissors directly on the spine of the book to make the weight the most it could be. "Go through and find any article that publishes my name. Don't miss a single one, because this is important." He flipped to a two-page article and pointed to his name scattered through it, then carefully cut and placed it on the postal scale. He pointed to the scale, then wrote the digital weight to one hundredth of a gram in a thick, heavy journal. "Do this each day, and add the total weights. That's what I want. A total weight of my press clippings each day to compare with the prior days."

Wilson knitted his brow.

The President looked deeply into Wilson's eyes. "Doesn't that make perfect sense to you? Most of our elected officials depend on ratings in national polls. But they lie about what polls say and interpret them however they want them to be. The liberal editors are pigheaded and don't like my progressive method of governing. Many have called me dictatorial. They lie with their one-sided polls to make me look bad. But I've got them by the tail on that. I look at the weights of all the press clippings, and if it's heavier than the prior day, that's good for my image. If the weight is lower, that means I must bang on my chest and give them more tweets to talk about."

"But, Mr. President, uh, there are news stories printed every day that, uh, fail . . . to render . . . the . . . the praise you deserve . . ." He paused when he saw The President frown and ball up his fists as his muscles tensed. Wilson quickly added, "A few stories, I might clarify."

A faint smile crossed The President's face. "I like the way you think, Will Thompson. I recall the words of Will Rogers, 'There's no such thing as bad press.' "

Wilson fell back slightly on his heels before saying, "Oh, I, uh, have no doubt Mr. Rogers said something like that, but P.T. B . . . Barnum originally coined that phrase, and it's a good one. And add to that, Oscar Wilde's quote: 'The only thing worse than being talked about is not being talked about.' That's exactly what you're doing with the weights of the news articles."

The President's face softened, then he smiled, and finally, he broke into a quiet laugh. "You know, that's really funny, Will Thompson. Give me another quote like that one."

Wilson took a deep breath as he realized that his potentially disastrous correction of The President just turned in his favor. Feeling a bit more confident, he asked, "How about the *Atlanta Confabulation* newspaper saying, 'All publicity is good, if it's intelligent'?"

The President frowned in a friendly manner as he stood, walked to Wilson, and placed his hand on his shoulder. "Write that down for me somewhere. I'll use that in a tweet the next time CNS gets under my skin."

Wilson was beginning to feel like a walking encyclopedia, much like he felt when he answered the many questions of his brothers and sisters, to whom he was their only father figure. Thinking of them, he laughed quietly and took a deep breath. *As a matter of fact, this is just like with the kids.* This thought placed him back home and in the presence of his siblings. *He's so much like them, I'll just treat him as such.* His tense muscles relaxed. His shaking stopped. He put aside the fact that he was giving instruction to a rich and powerful man. He felt at ease with the intensity of the discussion as he said, with a smile, “Here's another, uh, P.T. Barnum quote that you might also use, 'No man ever went broke overestimating the ignorance of the American public,' or 'Without publicity, a terrible thing happens. Nothing.' ”

The President gave a quiet, “Ha, ha, ha,” smiled, and squeezed Wilson's shoulder. “What you are saying justifies the job I am giving you: That there's no harm inflicted on me by the negative press their ‘false news’ reports bring. Whatever they write, I continue to refute their claims, and that gets more pages written about me, pushing the daily weight total up. As your quotes imply, the more the weight of the clippings, the more popular I am. Doesn't that make sense to you?”

Wilson held his shoulders high. “Yes, sir. I will be honored to be of service to you.”

“And don’t forget to get good, three-inch filet mignons. That black eye looks terrible.”

Chapter 6

Two weeks later.
A tiny, square office next to the Oval Office

Every day after that, for two weeks, Wilson left his Capitol job at 5 pm, retrieved the news articles, and returned to his makeshift office in the White House, one with a Power Pet automatic pet door at the bottom. The desk was so small, Wilson wondered if the prior dogs in that office, Bobo and Sunshine, used that for their correspondence. He squeezed onto a well-cushioned office chair that supported only half of his butt. Obviously, it had been the property of some past president's child. There, he cut clippings and recorded their weight. This job took a lot of time, so much that he usually slept on the blue sofa in the West Wing lobby. He used the 4'x4' shower concealed behind a wall in the visitor's bathroom. Rarely did he get to sleep by 2 am. He was up every day at 5 am, showered, dressed in a laundered (by the White House staff) brightly colored golf shirt and khaki pants, and then ate a breakfast energy bar. At 5:30, he took the clippings and the recording book to The President. On Saturday and Sunday, he took a twenty-minute bus ride to sleep at night in his garage apartment in southeast Washington, DC. Despite the grueling schedule, Wilson bounded from the sofa each morning with a smile and a skip to his walk.

Wilson couldn't help but scan-read the articles he clipped, and it didn't take but a couple hours on this new job to see the wisdom of The President's clip-and-weigh assignment. Eighty percent of the writings were critical of his actions. On his first day, he counted twelve opposing his use of the social media to spontaneously express ideas about his plans for national policy. The writers didn't state their party affiliation, except one; the Republican governor of Indiana, Cliff Halfcocked. He said these matters should be discussed and formulated by his cabinet and the many highly paid political advisors, not by tweets in the middle of the night. Ted Darnitt, a writer from Atlanta's *Patchwork Paper*, decried The President's snap Twitter decisions on major issues that affected millions of people both in America and all over the world. He gave in-house statistics which showed that not only did the Democrats oppose "Twitter Politics," a small but growing number of his own party faithful did also. There were no articles that supported The President's Twitter position. Was reading these derogatory remarks so painful that The President studied the weights rather than the content of the news reports?

Wilson stopped his reading and thought, *Wow, how hard it must be for even the most confident person in the world to read all this critical material every day and still function.*

The more clips that Wilson read, the more obvious it was that The President's response to negative publicity was to rebuke his critics immediately and repeatedly, even members of his White House staff whom he'd appointed, often hinting that he would fire them. He gave the label "false news" to reports that voiced any opposition of his proposals. Wilson was beginning to understand The President a little better as he continued to read of the long-time *Washington Unposted* columnist George Willsay repudiating The President's nullification of international treaties signed by previous presidents. "This makes the United States unreliable in fulfilling its commitments to other nations," Willsay stated. Other prominent political analysts, Woodshed and Barnstorm, lashed out at the use of "Executive Privilege" to skirt issues not backed by Congress. Wilson scribbled on his notepad to look up "Executive Privilege" in the library. He recalled his recent study of the Electoral College as he read that Virginia's Democratic Senators, Warnher and Kaintsay, criticized it for giving the election to The President rather than the Democratic candidate, Hilda Bendover, who garnered the majority of the popular vote. Wilson chuckled to himself. *Too bad Willsay and Kaintsay don't get Warnher to Bendover and accept the election results.*

In his readings, it occurred to him that any group which asked the opinions of ten people immediately formulated a national poll which they rushed to publish. This multitude of polls was consistent in showing The President's forty percent approval rating and that he remained extremely popular among his followers: The supporters liked the way he remained adamant about his campaign promises and bulldozed paths to instate them. They said they loved a person who was strong enough to battle the Washington establishment.

One of The President's biggest issues, if not THE biggest, was his proposed Great Wall of America to block one hundred percent of border crossing from Mexico. This garnered dozens of critical op-eds. Wilson was amused at finding a solitary supporter of The Great Wall of America; a dubious compliment from Bigger Glascock of the Butterflies Be Banished Society. Glasscock defended The Great Wall of America, saying that "Vegetation providing butterfly sanctuary would be destroyed by The Great Wall of America, further blocking Mexican Migrant Monarchs from crossing the Texas border." He stated that they smothered his Choke Cherry trees on the Rio Grande, dropping his income from $2,500 to $2,250 this year. Wilson laughed and said aloud, "I'll make sure The President reads this. He'll eat it up."

Despite being part of the White House team, Wilson had to agree with reports that The President was narcissistic. Though he hadn't known him long, he had already observed that his need for admiration was not only excessive but also somewhat comical. One New York reporter, Cherry Benhad, suggested that narcissism gave him power to circumvent any need to please everybody.

Wilson nodded as he thought, *His intolerance of criticism must give him the motivation to accomplish some of his unpopular goals. And his strong sense of entitlement must make him feel there are no roadblocks that he couldn't blast away in Superman-like daring. Yes, others are critical of the overt narcissism, but this is also the backbone of his power. His fans love it.*

Chapter 7

5:30 am a week later. The Oval Office

These thoughts about the pros and cons of The President's narcissism were still on his mind as Wilson knocked and entered the Oval Office. He was surprised as a jovial President bounded from his desk and greeted him with, "Will Thompson, you should have been with me last night. I had the greatest campaign rally in Georgia."

"Uh, campaign rally?"

"Well, no, I guess I can't actually call it a campaign rally, being over two years 'til the election, so call it my policy review with my great Augusta, Georgia, electorate. Over fifty thousand there, yelling and screaming good things about me. I love it when I can attract bigger crowds than even the biggest rock stars. Made me feel good."

"Augusta, Georgia? Uh, you didn't go there to play golf at the Augusta Nationwide, did you?"

"Well, yes. But that wasn't my primary motive for going there. Well, maybe it wasn't," he said, as his voice trailed off. "My score was perfect anyway. I beat Tig Forest and Teddy Mickleburger, both Masters champs, and one US Open champ, Booking Copcatcher. Jesus, I'm a good golfer. Do you have more good news for me today?"

Wilson frowned. The news was mostly critical, but after a second, he realized the intent of the question. His face lit up. "Oh, uh . . . yes, sir. Three thousand six hundred twenty-eight point seven hundred forty-two grams. That's just a little over eight pounds. Your biggest score ever."

A smiling President took the weight log from Wilson. After a prolonged eye-to-eye stare, he said, even though Wilson's black eye was long gone, "Get a couple more fillets. The eye still looks awful," then opened the log to the day's page. He bowed his head over it and viewed the figures up close. "Hmm," he said, as he ran his finger slowly along the columns of figures. After several minutes of scrutiny, he closed the book. "This is good. I won't have to waste time with extra tweets today."

"Yes, sir. You have extra time for another round of golf. Are, uh, you thinking of Pebbly Beach? That course is beautiful."

The President spoke quietly. "I don't like California that much. They're so liberal, they'd vote for a billy goat over any Republican. Make a note for me to call Jack Nickelface to see if we can move the Pebbly Beach course to a nice place, like Coney Island or Atlantic City."

Wilson wrote a note on his pad at The President's request. He shook his head in disbelief at what the man just said, then absentmindedly scribbled a note in his own words, "Does this guy have a gourd for a brain?" He doodled on the writing pad and then watched as The Man cracked open a can of Diet Coke and sipped. Wilson interrupted another uncomfortable period of silence to ask The President's opinion of the Electorial College. "I . . . I've been doing extra reading on the Electoral College, and I wondered . . ."

"Yes, yes, the Electoral College. A great amendment to the Constitution."

Wilson paused with an open mouth a few seconds as he recalled his readings in the library. "Uh, yes. The twenty-third amendment that gave Washington, DC three electoral votes and made them a part of the election system."

"What about the rest of the states?"

"Uhh, it's just as you said. That was spelled out in the main body of the Constitution."

The President listened to these words with his lips parted and one eye half-closed. "Yes, yes. I knew that." Then he stood stiffly erect as a confident look came over his face. "I am so proud of my great victory, even though I never really understood why the Electoral College gave California fifty-five votes and Texas thirty-six votes with Montana and North Dakota having only three each. If Executive Privilege would allow, I'd reverse those numbers. I like Montana and the Dakotas, and as I already said, I don't give a fig about California, and Texas is too hot for golf this time of year."

Wilson was dumbfounded. *Just as I'm beginning to understand a little of the mental workings of The Man, he says something totally stupid. What goes on in this guy's mind?* He swallowed as he backed to the door while saying, "Enjoy the golf course."

The President walked quickly to the door. Wilson held out his hand, expecting to shake, but The President put both his hands behind his back as he said, "What do you think you are doing, Will, Thompson? Don't touch me. Shaking hands is filthy. I must teach our CDC to make that a priority — to show America how bad hand-shaking is. It spreads millions of germs, and I certainly don't want any germs from someone insignificant who works under me."

Wilson thought about how he had been the one correcting The President's lack of knowledge of even the most basic facts, which intensified the fury he felt at being called insignificant. He turned, with heavy veins bulging on his now-fiery-red face, and stormed from the room. He took several long steps before stopping, turning around, and bursting into the office again. With his hands on his hips and leaning toward The President, he screamed, "Y . . . y . . . you're rich and I am poor. Yes, I'm working my tail off to support my mother and six sibs. Y . . . you've sat on your rear-end paying us 'street people' your father's money so we can make you great, and you dare look at us as 'underlings'!" He grabbed an armful of the articles he'd clipped. "Take these and shove them up your gold-plated pipes! And pay some other 'insignificant underling' like me to do this job and wipe it so your hands won't get any germs from your sterile ass!" He threw the articles all over the office and reached for the door. "I . . . I. . . I'm outta here!"

As he did so, The President jumped beside him and snatched the note about the call to Nickelface. Wilson grabbed for the note that would cost him his job were the job not already lost. The President leaned back and jerked, tearing the note in half. Wilson felt momentary euphoria as he ran from the office carrying half of his original note. Halfway down the hall, he looked at it. "Call Nickelface about moving Pebbly Beach." That was all. "Dammit," he mumbled.

Even knowing he couldn't go back to retrieve the other half of the note, Wilson was proud that he had finally stood up and didn't back down. The pride overcame the remorse of throwing away his job. He went to his tiny office to take away his toothbrush and two changes of clothes he'd been keeping there. He'd need them for job hunting tomorrow if The President had him also fired from the maintenance staff at the Capitol Building.

Before he could exit, Wilson was intercepted in his office by a black-suited Diet Coke carrier. “Here’s a note from Mr. President, sir.”

“Sir?” Wilson asked aloud.

“It’s important that you read this immediately, sir.”

Wilson saw something unusual: a handwritten note bearing The President’s signature. *He never writes. All his communications are typed . . . or tweeted.* He took a deep breath. And read: “Thank you so much for all the wonderful weights and refresher history lessons you offer. And I thought you might need the other half of your note. You have gumption and moxie. I love it. See you tomorrow morning at 5:30 am sharp!”

Wilson turned the paper over and read the words he’d written on the note pad: “Does this guy have a gourd for a brain?” He crumpled the note and stuffed it in his pocket.

<u>Chapter 8</u>

9 pm four days later.
The basement of the Capitol Building

Wilson had just clipped and weighed all The President's printed news stories and was checking on his work at the Capitol Building. At a distance he saw a door open slightly. Two eyes gazed out. On seeing Wilson, the door closed. Wilson looked straight ahead as he continued walking, pretending not to have seen this. After passing the door where the peeker had been, he then walked beyond his destination toward a hallway to his right into which he turned, walked a few paces, then tiptoed back. He peeked around the corner. After a minute, a first face appeared, that of Democratic Senator Dick Rubbing. Next was a person with his suit jacket pulled up around his head. Despite the disguise, Wilson thought he recognized him as Democratic Congressman Rich Boozer from Arkansas. “Oops,” Boozer said, as he bumped into the wall. Boozer pulled the jacket below his eye level and continued walking.

Joining the two was Hawaii's Republican Representative, Ima Wright. The three walked hurriedly away in the opposite direction. Wilson kept in a shadow as he watched for a few minutes. Another head bobbed from another door, looked both ways, then tiptoed after the others. It was the Democrat Johnnie Crapper. Just before the long corridor took a right turn, Boozer opened the door of a closet and popped inside. Crapper followed.

Wilson was familiar with that space. It was scarcely twenty feet long and ten feet wide, with shelves at the back and one sidewall filled with thousands of reams of computer paper, hundreds of boxes of ballpoint pens, white-out correction fluid, pencils, erasers, and all sorts of office supplies that he used in his daily work.

Wilson started toward his office when another man appeared, the House Democrat Marty Canttell, walking on his tiptoes to follow the others into the closet. What was happening? This was a scene quite similar to the one previously described by his co-worker. *What's this all about?* Wilson shrugged. *Democrats and a Republican, together, in a secret meeting? They can't agree on anything.* Wilson's curiosity was high. He walked into an adjacent room and put his ear to the ventilation duct that supplied both rooms. He could well hear the people milling around.

Inside the dimly lit storage closet, the five people gathered to discuss their clandestine purpose. Rubbing walked to the light switch and turned it off, leaving only an inch square night light to provide the faintest of illumination. He muttered, “I don't want any hidden cameras recording any of this.” He turned to the others and asked, “Does anyone else know of our meeting today?”

Boozer answered. “Jesus. I would think many others feel as we do, but this is a serious, as well as an important, issue. I know I can trust you fellows, but I wouldn't trust my fate to anybody else in DC. There's a big time jail sentence awaiting if they learn we're even talking about this.”

Ima Wright asked in her soft, musical voice, “Are we certain there are no bugs?”

“A hunnert percent sure,” Crapper followed. “I checked it with this.” He raised his hand to show a hand-sized, electronic device with a chrome-plated, foot-and-a-half long telescoping antenna.

"Ouch! You poked me in the butt."

"Madam, I was just trying to show you."

"Show us in the dark? You crazy?" Wright asked.

"Sorry about that, Ima."

"Stop it! Stop it! Let's get down to business.," Marty Canttell said. "That bug detector's not traceable, is it?"

"No. Got it from a pawn shop."

"What? They'll recognize you as a 'White House-er' anywhere in this city!" Rubbing cried out.

"It's OK, it's OK. I had my wife do it. And she used her own credit card."

"Oh. That's alright then."

Rich Boozer spoke: "Did you check his health records?"

Rubbing's pronounced head nodding went unseen in the darkness. "They're on public record. We received no help there. He'll live 'til he's a hundred, if his doctor doesn't lie about stuff too."

Wright said, “But he has to be eliminated! We need him gone in order to get this country back on track again. The House, with its Democratic majority, can’t agree on anything, not even The President’s Great Wall of America. And the House Speaker won’t bring impeachment up for a vote and even refuses to discuss the other avenue of dismissal, declaring The President incapable of leading the country. These are the only two legal procedures for removing him from office, with the next election being two years away. But another thing to consider is not at all legal . . .”

Canttell spoke quickly, “Are you suggesting assass . . .”

Rubbing countered, “Alright, no need to talk dirty. There’s a lady present, and there’s no need to say it twice.”

“No, Rubbing, he's choking on the word 'assassination'.”

Canttell told them, “Oh. That's big. But we can't say that word. I was a deputy in the CIA . . .”

"Half of the White House staff held that title: Deputy in the CIA. The other half was Deputy in the FBI," Boozer chugged.

"Shut up. I'm talking!"

"I didn't want the FBI or the CIA."

"So?"

"I wanted to play baseball."

"So, Boozer, why didn't you continue with baseball rather than going into government?"

"I couldn't hit."

All was quiet for a minute before Canttell continued. "As I was saying, I was in the FBI before I became a senator."

"Let's don't go through that again."

"Ok, ok, ok. In the FBI . . ."

"I thought it was the CIA."

Canttell jumped up and down and pulled at his hair, then brushed his suit coat before taking a couple deep breaths. "You nitwits could drive a guy crazy."

"Like The President did with Emerson and Higgenblooper?"

"That's Higgenlooper."

"Yes. The FBI."

"No. CIA."

"Yes. They encouraged the replacement of that politically insensitive word with erased, nullified, eliminated, withdrawn, silenced, or subjugated."

Boozer said, "My coach at Michigan — when I was the star linebacker and on the All-Conference team three years in a row — used the word 'sideline' when he wanted us to kill . . ."

"Shhh!"

Boozer lowered his voice and said, "Ok. He told me to 'sideline' a Washington quarterback that was scoring on us in the '78 Rose Bowl, when I . . ."

"Boozer, I didn't mean shhh, quiet. I meant shhh, enough of football. This is serious business . . . No matter how we say it, it's dangerous. If we get caught, it's a long time in prison. We need to know there's no other alternative."

"Uh oh."

Wright, in her quiet voice, said, "And Mary Surratt was hanged just for *helping* Booth after *he* shot Lincoln, and she had absolutely *nothing* to do with it."

"But The President's got to go! We are patriots, and the people that elected us want us to protect them from a leader so erratic that he continues to make hurried decisions which harm us all. We're here because Congress has been slack. For Chrissake, they don't even try to charge him with contempt of Congress . . ."

Wright interrupted Crapper with, "And they ignore his collusion with foreign nations in the election that made him The President. That's certainly an impeachable offense. And it's not just the House Speaker that's failed to act. So many in Congress are afraid of impeachment."

Boozer spoke loudly, "But there's no reason to go the impeachment route. It wouldn't make a difference. We have enough Republicans in the Senate to overturn Congress' vote for impeachment, and The President would use that to his advantage, boasting that he beat Congress again."

Rubbing gritted his teeth. "I want him out, and his impeachment will gift the country with a Democratic majority that we can enjoy for years to come, just as it was at times in the thirties, forties, fifties, and sixties. It was great when, back then, we Democrats controlled everything: the House, the Senate, the Presidency, the Supreme Court, the majority of federal judges, and every other appointed office in the country."

"You're right."

"No, she's Ima Wright. And I'm Dick Rubbing."

"How could anyone from Hawaii be named Ima Wright? That sounds more Irish than Hawaiian."

Wright spoke. "Actually, my husband is Irish, but my maiden name was Wong."

Rubbing replied, "But if it was wrong, why didn't you have the name changed?"

Ima snapped back, "No, dummy. Wong, Wong, Wong!"

"Are you saying that three wrongs make a Wright? My biology teacher never taught me that."

Rubbing shook as he laughed, and Wright reacted to the ribaldry with an eyeroll.

Boozer chuckled, as he stated, "You guys are a piece of work. I hope your constituents are smarter than their representatives."

Canttell stomped the floor. "Alright, stop the nonsense. Let's get back to business. While Republicans and

Democrats battle one another, The President could get mad at the Iranians in one of his little fits and push that big red button on his desk to launch atomic bombs and destroy the entire Planet Earth, and I don't mean the button for Diet Cokes."

Raising her voice a little higher, Wright interjected, "Dick's onto something. That's why you Dems can't do anything. I'm a Republican, and you're just pushing this for your own party's benefit, ignoring that I even chose to meet with you! Think more about the effect presidential 'subjugation', or whatever, will have on *the nation! Not your own party*! You guys are the reason there's no bipartisan compromising!"

Dick Rubbing came in again. "We need to act and act now. Let's 'subjugate' The President and take control of our own future, and if we get caught, we'll just accept our punishment. Just as Patrick Henry said, 'Give me liberty or give me death.' "

Wright rubbed her throat. "But I don't want to be hanged."

Crapper tooted, "They won't hang us, even if they learn who we are. We'll be national heroes."

"You mean with ticker tape parades and all?"

"Dummy. Ticker tape parades ended years ago. They use confetti now."

"Then I wouldn't be much of a hero without ticker tape. I'm out," Ima said.

Two others followed her out the door into the hallway as Crapper said after them, "Looks like I'll have to do it by myself. But I'll tell them all of you were co-conspirators."

The departing group put on brakes and turned. Wright said, "Johnnie Crapper, you aren't dragging us into one of your harebrained schemes . . ."

"Like your 'hundreds' of bills that die in committees," Boozer added. "We're not going to share guilt with you on *anything*."

"Then give me some help. Propose a method of 'sidelining' him so the Veep can take his place. He's good at being bipartisan. And then we'd finally be able to work with the White House and get the country back on track."

Boozer paused and then said the words, "Poison. Russian Wackem."

"Yeah. That's a good way."

"And it'll make him fall dead with no suffering, so my Russian friends say."

"Yes. The Russians are bumping off their political enemies with poisons right and left, and they've never been caught. They did another one last week."

Boozer pondered for a moment and then spoke. "Say, I drink with three or four Russians at the Congressional Pubber every Tuesday and Friday. The guy rumored to be in charge of one of the recent Russian poisonings is a good friend of mine. He's a real nice guy."

"A nice guy? That bumps off people with poison? Are you nuts?"

Wright shrugged. "That's OK with me, so long as he acts friendly. We need to do this. Ask him if he'd like the job."

"I already asked. The Wackem he used in his last four kills is being investigated by Scotland Yard. He said that each batch of the drug has distinctive features that can be traced to the source, so their big Wackem Factory in Vladivostocking is under scrutiny. Too bad. They had to lay off fifty thousand workers and temporarily close shop til it all blows over. That was a real blow to their local economy, like our shutting down the steel mills in Pittsburgh."

"So, why'd you even bring up the subject?"

"Oh, yes. My friend says they're using a new poison, one made from scorpion fish in an Oriental lab. He'll sell us enough to kill one guy for fifty G's and give us a written, money-back guarantee."

"Hey, 'Oriental' is in that group of words we're not supposed to say. Asian is proper."

"Oh, right. And I wouldn't want Congresswoman Allover Courts on my case."

Another voice spoke. "Fifty G's is cheap. I can get that much from my campaign money."

"How will you avoid being caught?"

"I'll just say I remodeled my office, like all three of you have done since last November's election. Fifty grand is only a drop in the bucket to what we all 'borrowed' from campaign finance dollars."

"But everybody says my office is the nicest in town, a lot nicer than yours."

"Really?"

"Yep. It has 24-carat gold faucets and shower-heads in my five bathrooms. And with rare, antique Oriental, uh, Asian, rugs throughout the fifteen rooms. Some of 'em cost forty grand apiece. And I get to take 'em with me when I retire."

"Fifteen rooms? How do you rate? My apartment just has nine."

"Just takes money."

"Maybe I'll have to do more remodeling and take over the adjacent apartment."

"That'll cost you a weekend fund-raising event. "

"I know. It makes it tough on a senator, to have to let my Little Honey be alone for a weekend just to appease my constituents."

"You mean your wife?"

"No. I always take my wife on fund-raisers. It looks good to the public to be a family man."

"Ok, Ok! Just cut the crap! The Russians know their stuff. Let's just do it, their way," was the response of Canttell.

"How will we gain the fifty thousand we need? I sure don't want to fork this out of my pocket."

"And I ain't crazy about tapping my campaign fund. When I get voted out because of this crazy president, I want to take all of that with me," Wright railed.

"Me too."

"Me too."

"Then can we put this on our travel allowance?"

"Travel allowance? You mean we have to go to Moscow to get it?"

"You're a complete idiot. They'll catch us at the airport with the drug and put us in jail, all without solving our 'Mr. President' problem."

"What about the Chinese? They're asking us to help appease The President so he won't block their missile base in the Sparsely Islands."

Rubbing started, "That's right! I'm a good friend of their State Council Premier, Chinchilla."

"Hah! It's Chuchin. And how can he be a 'close friend' and you not even know his correct name?"

"I was close, anyway."

"Close, but no cigar," Canttell told.

"Did you know that 'close' is only important in horseshoes?"

"How about hand grenades?"

No one laughed.

"Well, I knew the Chinese man had a name like some kinda dog."

"Okay, okay. Chuchilla is an important man . . ."

"Chuchin. He's a person who is well regarded in China, so treat him with respect, and learn how to say his name."

"Ok, ok, ok. We all know the Chinese are generous with their money when it comes to our helping their political causes."

"Well, there's a twelve-hour time differential, so it's 10:30 am in Beijing, so call him now."

"Let me call right now." Rubbing lifted his burner phone and made the call. After ten minutes, Rubbing hung up and said, "Done deal. The Chinese came through. We'll have the fifty grand in four days, in cash. Boozer, when we get the money, you're elected to negotiate with the Russians."

"Gotcha."

Wilson ducked his head and moved down the side hall quickly as the closet door opened and the men and woman left, one by one. He hadn't heard every word that was spoken, but what was clear was that this was primarily a group of Democrats with a Republican, finally agreeing on something. But Wilson was troubled. Had he really just listened to the formulation of a plan to bring harm to his friend, The President? *I'll have to keep an eye and an ear out to be certain of what this is all about.*

Chapter 9

9 pm a week later. The Congressional Pubber

A briefcase-carrying congressman, Rich Boozer built his confidence with a double vodka martini at the bar before going to the table with his Russian acquaintance, Vladimir Vladimir Slapavich. He sat down and ordered a second double before getting to the usual barroom chit-chat. The Russian with the greying crew cut wore a thin, pastel blue T-shirt that spotlighted his muscular chest and arms. He spoke in broken English. Vladimir Vladimir Slapavich claimed to be an executive in an investment firm in Zurich.

The American's speech began to slur before he was ready to ask the question. He leaned close and whispered in Slapavich's ear. "I have the money. Do you have that drug?"

"Oh yes, my comrade. Well, when the dollars are in the pocket of my Russian knock-off Wranglers, the drug will be yours," he said in a heavy Russian accent.

"I have the money in cash, here," Boozer whispered, raising the briefcase.

"Money in briefcases is only done in movies. I don't want cash. I need your check. I work with Americans all the time in my business." He reached into the pocket of his skin-tight jeans and produced his business card, giving his name and information concerning the EAFA Investment Company. "My business is reputable, and I handle investments of many of your colleagues on Capitol Hill. Right now, I'm growing several campaign funds for your elected officials."

What's EAFA stand for?"

"Eastern Alliance to Fuck America."

Boozer rocked back on his heels and opened his lips to retaliate but thought better of it, and the only words that he could say were, "Ok. Do you have the drug?"

"The scorpion fish poison? Yes. I always have the drug. I could get a call from my colleagues to eliminate an enemy any time, even today. Write me the check and I will get the merchandise from my Jaguar."

"Agreed."

The congressman wrote the check payable to EAFA Investment Company from his personal account, post-dated it five days, and passed it on to the Russian with the stipulation, "Don't cash it for a week. I need to deposit this money in my account Monday, and it takes a couple of days before it can be honored by my bank. But I assure you, the check will be valid."

"I trust you, just as you know that if the money is not there, scorpion fish will be listed as your cause of death."

Boozer swallowed. "I can assure you. Just save your scorpion fish for another of your enemies."

The Russian laughed. "I trust you." He passed to the congressman a Russian briefcase containing a heavily wrapped package the size of a cigar box.

"We always transport this with an ounce of marijuana scattered in the wrapping. If you get caught, just confess to pot possession. They'll smell it and book you on the lesser charge."

"Whoa! I don't want to get caught with anything."

"It won't happen, but if it does, you have an out."

"Is that my only fear?"

"Just be careful, my friend. It is more powerful than Wackem. Wear thick gloves and a substantial face mask. This stuff will penetrate the skin of your hand and kill you within minutes. Inhaled, you'll be dead in seconds. I want you alive to make another purchase."

Rich Boozer, now pale and trembling, looked at the package and then at the Russian. "Is it safe to carry it?"

"Yes. So long as it doesn't get wet in a rainstorm or you touch the actual powder."

"And how do you say I use it, to get a certain kill?"

"Put a spoonful in his coffee, tea, or vodka."

"Vodka?"

"Doesn't everybody drink vodka?"

"No."

"You Americans are funny people like that."

"But, our man's so fearful of being poisoned, he won't let anybody even get near his food, let alone put stuff in it."

"In that case, moisten a small paint brush with water, dip it in the scorpion fish powder, and paint it on a door handle, a menu at a restaurant, his daily newspaper, or anything he handles. But be careful to wear gloves and a mask when you handle in any manner. It kills by lung exposure quicker than through the skin. I guarantee success."

Boozer walked away, with a briefcase in each hand, continually bumping into the wall due to his listing to the left from the heavy load of money overbalancing the light case of poison.

Chapter 10

10 pm the next Monday. Same supply closet in the same basement of the same Capitol Building

The group huddled around Boozer as he told of the purchase. "It was easy," Boozer stated. "He gave no hassle. He just took my check and gave me scorpion fish poison."

"I expected he'd try to jack up the price."

"Well, he threatened to put some on me if the check was void in any way."

"That didn't scare you?"

"Well, yes. I didn't sleep a wink all weekend and was at the bank the first thing today to be certain the Chinese cash was in my account. Whew. The Russians know how to scare a guy."

"Can we see what we got for China's money?"

"It's all wrapped up, but I brought gloves. I'm sort of curious as to what it looks like too. It's dangerous to touch it, so stand back and let me unwrap it."

Boozer snapped open his briefcase, revealing the rectangular package with a heavy brown paper wrapping. As he removed one layer of paper, the smell of cannabis filled the room.

"Nice," Rubbing said.

Boozer then removed a second and a third wrap before, at last, the box was exposed. They all stood in reverence, observing the oversized cigar box emblazoned with the hammer and sickle symbol.

Canttell punched Boozer in the ribs. "Go on. Open the box."

Boozer looked around at the others.

"Get on with it," another said. "We aren't going to touch it, or even get close." As he said this, they all took a giant step backwards.

Boozer, with gloved hands, touched the box.

Wright cringed.

Boozer positioned his fingers on the lid of the box.

"Are there cigars in the box? I like the Russian Black cigars."

"Yuck. Those Russian Black smokes are so strong they make my toes curl."

"Curly toes? They'd look good on you, Ima."

Wright rolled her eyes. Crapper gasped. Rubbing stepped back farther.

"Is it a powder or liquid?"

"Powder."

Rubbing took another step back.

Boozer opened the box slowly.

First one, then the others, inched forward toward the cigar box.

Canttell leaned forward for a closer look, then another did the same.

Everyone held their breath as they saw the contents of the fifty-grand box. It was half-filled with tan granules that gleamed in the dim light of the room.

"They're pretty," Wright said.

"Not half as pretty as your curly toenails."

Before anyone could say another word, Canttell placed his finger under his nose and suddenly lurched forward toward the cigar box. His loud, "ACHOO!" echoed in the small room. Tan granules flew into the air, glittering in every corner of the tiny room.

Boozer shouted his words of apology: "I'm sorry, I forgot about the masks. We're all gonna die!"

Chapter 11

7 am the next day.
A very tiny office next to the Oval Office

Wilson read the headline in the next day's *Un-posted* newspaper: POISON PASSED IN RUSSIAN POT. He shook his head as he read the brief article: "Quick action by four Democratic senators and one Republican likely saved the lives of hundreds in the Capitol Building yesterday when they alertly nabbed a suspicious package suspected to contain some deadly drug mixed with marijuana. They carried it to an isolated basement closet before opening. Hundreds of Capitol Hill personnel were spared contact with the poison by the heroic deeds of Democratic Congressmen Rich Boozer, Johnny Crapper, and Marty Canttell, who, along with Republican Ima Wright and the big hero of the day, Senator Rubbing, are in the Walter Reed Army Hospital undergoing treatment. They are expected to survive, though it could be weeks before they can return home. All five members, including Dick Rubbing, will continue in Congress."

Wilson sat up in his office chair. *Oh, my God! That was poison intended for The President! And I heard the plans but did nothing to stop them!* He closed his eyes and wrung his hands. *Hopefully, no one else will attempt such a thing, but if they do, I must be decisive in my actions.*

Chapter 12

**Four hours later the same day.
The Chinese Embassy in DC**

"Hello, Premier Chuchin. This is Ambassador Wu in Washington. I have great news for you. The Americans are dumb as . . . how do you say 'chicken shit' in Chinese?"

"Ji la shi."

"Yes. They took our $50,000 US dollars and paid that to the Russians for one ounce of our . . . how do you say 'scorpion fish poison' in Chinese?"

"Duo ci yu."

"Yes. So the Russians pay us $50,000 US dollars to get them another 320 more ounces of duo ci yu. So, the Russians gouge the Americans for poison to kill their wicked comrades, and we get free American help for the Sparsely Islands."

"Yes, Ambassador Wu, you are right. The Americans *are* dumb as ji la shi."

Chapter 13

7 pm a week later. A familiar bench beside a familiar newsstand outside the familiar Capitol Building

Wilson had finished his work at the Capitol and relaxed while eating his peanut butter sandwich and reading *Screw The Press* magazine. There was yet another celebrity voicing criticism of The President. As he turned a page in the dim evening light, he glimpsed a short, chubby, middle-aged man with rosy cheeks and a double chin wearing a brown Brooks Brothers trench coat, hurrying down the other side of the street. It was an exceptionally warm evening in this mid-season for such a heavy garment. Moreover, the man's sunglasses were certainly out of place at this hour. Wilson held the magazine toward the fellow and peeked over it.

Looking close, he recognized the familiar face of Republican Senator Ben Wilting, chairman of the finance committee. He carried a heavy grocery bag. Wilson was curious. With the other strange happenings in DC, he chose to investigate. Keeping at a comfortable distance from Wilting, he followed.

He watched as, two blocks away, the man ducked into the shadows between two buildings, put on a wide-brimmed hat and sunglasses taken from a Big Hats For Big-Headed People bag, and replaced them with his red and green checkered bow tie and the coat. He tucked the bag with his garments under a box in the alley, then lifted his cumbersome grocery bag.

Wilson blended in with the pedestrian traffic as Wilting stopped at the door of a dingy pawn shop, looked from side to side, peered over his sunglasses, then entered.

Wilson followed Wilting inside the pawn shop and pretended to look at a rack of guitars in the front of the shop.

The senator looked straight ahead, marched to the rear of the store, ducked through a cloth partition behind the sales desk, and entered the private office behind, breathing laboriously and panting from exertion.

Wilson moved to the back of the shop and tried to listen to the conversation.

Senator Wilting spoke softly, as if his hand covered his mouth. "Oliver?"

"No. Iluva Singha," the owner spoke with a loud, booming voice. He was a bald-headed, dark-skinned man with an obese frame wearing a wrinkled, open-collared dress suit with an untied black tie draped around his neck. Sitting at a desk covered with dozens of folders and loose papers, he reached his hand into an opened desk drawer, grasped an unnaturally shiny, black, oversized semi-automatic pistol, and slapped it on the desk. Without releasing his hand from the gun, he greeted Wilting in a staccato Indian accent. "Do you have the money?"

The buyer reached into his brown bag and pulled out hands full of money rolls. "You wanted one million Indian rupees." He pushed the rolls of bills toward the pistol. "Here it is; a million rupees in 200-rupee notes, five thousand of them. They were difficult to locate. Just why do you want your money in bulky stacks of rupees when it's so easy to handle the only $14,500 in US dollars?"

Ignoring the question, Singha began the arduous chore of unrolling and counting each bill. He looked up after this ten-minute chore. “You're an honorable man. It's all there. So many try to cheat me of one or two bills” He lifted his gun. The buyer began to sweat. As he moved to replace it in his desk drawer, his finger accidentally touched the trigger; a loud *BANG!* issued.

Senator Wilting dropped to his knees and clutched his chest.

Singha blew the smoke from the barrel as he held the weapon close to his face for inspection.

Wilting looked first at his hand, then his chest. There was no blood. He stood slowly.

“No worry, my friend, I bought this from Toys Are You-all, before the franchise closed. My roll of caps has just about expended. I must replace them,” Singha said, as he smiled and returned the “look-like” weapon to its drawer.

Wilting sighed with relief as Singha stood and waddled to a wall safe and removed a package the size of a sleeve of golf balls. He placed it in a paper bag and folded the top around the package.

Wilting took the bag. “A question. Where do you get this poison?”

Singha looked around, then whispered, "My son went to India last year. He climbed Strikeout Ignition shrubs and plucked the beans, then cut away the twenty-five seeds imbedded in each bean and ground them into a fine powder. These seeds contain Strictnun in its purest form. He brought me a satchel full. It's popular in your country for killing . . . rats. I think my preparation will take care of your . . . rats."

"Oh."

"And you inquired why I requested this odd payment? Well, I promised my wife I'd make a sale for a million today."

"Now, that's cheating on your wife. She thinks you mean a million American bucks."

"No," he said, with a boisterous laugh. "Thank God, she still hasn't adapted to American culture. She thinks she's still in India, and with our voluminous sack of rupees, she'll lay them all out on her bed and roll in them before going out and buying a new dress. She'll be really good to me tonight."

"How do you recommend I use the stuff? I'm certain it tastes bad."

"It does indeed. It's extremely bitter, but it takes only a tiny amount to do its intended job. A quarter of a teaspoon full will kill the biggest of . . . of rats. Place it in a drug capsule, have the victim inhale it in its powder form, or mix it with foods until it tastes palatable."

"But on the latter, how do I do that without killing myself getting the right taste?"

Find yourself a dog. Dogs' tastes are quite similar to a human. Let one sample it. If it shies away, either dilute it more or mix it with something else."

"Won't it kill the dog?"

"No, no. Not if you're careful. A big dog will gulp it down. Just use a small, feisty dog that touches new food items with its tongue before eating it. A lick of the surface won't bother it at all."

Wilson turned his back as the senator left the building. He had heard every word: Wilting bought Strict-nun, a rat poison commonly recently used in half a dozen homicides in the US and Canada. *Why would he have needed to disguise his face if he was truly only buying a rat killer? Was this going to be another attempt on The*

President's life? It was common knowledge in Washington that Senator Wilting was a loner. He was known as a good negotiator in the Democratic party when it came to most legislative decisions, but this was a President with whom one couldn't negotiate. Was this a revenge for the uncooperative nature of The President? Or some override of a deeply ingrained political allegiance to the nation that he must 'bypass' this man? Just planning a political assassination would be unlawful. *This is a successful politician with a lot to lose if his plot is discovered,* Wilson thought. *Just like Rubbing and Boozer's group. Why are these people making such a gamble? Do they feel The President is such a threat to America's future they'll lay everything on the line to be rid of him? Like the American Colonists during the Revolutionary War? Wilting's motivation would have to be strong to proceed in such a manner.*

Chapter 14

2 pm one week later. Wilting's Withering Willows home on Pooks Hill Road

Wilting left his office early to babysit his three-year-old granddaughter one afternoon while his wife and daughter went shopping. After the little girl was sound asleep in her afternoon nap, Wilting took the drug to his basement and mixed a quarter teaspoon of it, first with an inch square of cheese spread, then another in a dollop of butter, and, finally, one in a spoonful of deviled ham. He placed them individually on small Cheez-It crackers and smiled as he looked at his creation. "Now, for a taste test," he said aloud.

He tiptoed back upstairs and quietly lifted his white with brown spots Pomeranian and returned to his "work area". The dog licked Wilting's face as he rubbed noses with his pet and whispered, "I love you, my silly little dog." He held the Pom at arm's length as he looked him in the eye and said quietly, "I just want you to taste my three goodie woodies. Just touch it with your tongue and tell me if it's good. It's poison, so I won't let you eat *any* of it. I don't want anything to make my puppy wuppy sick."

With his left hand held firmly around the Pom's neck, he placed the butter square a foot from the dog's face. The Pom leaned to the cracker, his tongue shot out and touched the butter, then he quickly withdrew the tongue with a scowl on his face. "Good boy, good boy," Wilting said, as he rubbed the dog's head before placing the cheese spread cracker before him. The Pom reacted in the same fashion.

Wilting kissed the dog's face and said," Good dog. You're really helping me. Now try my hammy wammy cracker and tell me if it tastes bad too."

Wilting lifted the deviled ham cracker and turned to see his granddaughter standing beside the dog. He opened his mouth in surprise as the girl snatched the cracker from his hand and shoved it in his mouth, saying, "You have a cracker, Grandpa."

Wilting dropped the dog, swallowing the ham cracker completely. Both his hands went to his mouth as he screamed, "Call 911! I've been poisoned!"

The first EMT that rushed in recognized the senator. "You're Wilting, aren't you, sir?"

The senator, lying on the floor and clutching his throat, screamed, "No! I'm not wilting! I'm dying, you freaking idiot! Get me to the hospital!"

The next day, the *Unposted*'s headline read: BEN WILTING BEEN POISONED. The short report told of the heroic actions of the three-year-old girl who called 911. "The authorities are searching for the alleged villain who allegedly placed an alleged substance, allegedly a poison, in alleged food, who could allegedly face prison time for an alleged attempted murder charge, the alleged police chief alleges."

Wilson read the article when he was looking for items regarding The President. *Uh oh,* he thought. *This sounds familiar. At least now he won't be able to harm The President.*

Chapter 15

8 pm four days later. US Capitol Building basement (the floor immediately under the first floor)

Wilson moved slowly along the hallways, intentionally looking for any more suspicious activities and wondering, *How many others in DC are planning to get rid of The President*?

Sure enough, over a five-minute period, he witnessed Transportation Secretary Harry Johns, Secretary of Defense Danny Dapper, Secretary of Homeland Security Skip Church, and Secretary of Health and Human Services Bab Babs Callins each walk down the hall, then look back and forth before entering the small women's bathroom, just as his janitor friend had described before.

Wilson moved close enough to listen.

In the pitch black, the four were meeting here again. He could hear the quiet voice of Danny Dapper saying, “The heart attack drug is Sucksina Coleye. It's commonly used at the onset of hospital surgery to paralyze all muscles to allow placing the anesthesia endotracheal tube in the trachea. Often, it's needed to immobilize muscle groups when the surgery demands, such as the breathing mechanism when thoracic surgeons perform pulmonary surgery. It's impossible for heart or lung operations to proceed with a patient actively breathing."

"Huh?" an unidentifiable voice Wilson couldn't recognize asked.

Wilson heard a familiar sound that was like someone shifting their weight on a commode seat. *That's weird. A group of four in a bathroom, and one of them is on the john.*

Then he heard clearly the voice of Dapper. "Sorry to be so technical. But the ability to breathe ceases. Immediately. He gasps for breath, clutches his chest, and tries to talk but can't. In two minutes, he blacks out and collapses. Everyone around thinks he's had a heart attack. The drug is completely untraceable in the blood at autopsy. It's the perfect 'heart attack'."

A squeaky voice that was unmistakably Callin's rang out. "But if someone beats on The President's chest like we see on TV sitcoms, or does the heinie lick maneuver, can't they bring him back?"

The distinct gravelly voice of Skip Church spoke. "Uh, Bab Babs, it's actually the Heimlich maneuver."

The sound of movement on a commode seat was the background of a voice that was recognizable as one who spoke earlier. "This is different. The heinie licking is used for someone who chokes while eating a piece of meat, not for heart attacks."

"Oh. I didn't know all that," was Callins' return.

A hoarse grunt was uttered from the gravelly-voiced Church.

Wilson imagined that Church's eyes would roll at such an air-headed remark.

The quiet voice of Dapper returned. "The procedure I refer to is cardiopulmonary resuscitation. A doctor or someone trained in this method could keep him alive with external heart massage and breathing into his lungs. But none of our group has ever attended the classes they give the members of Congress each year. They all say they took the course, but they, like me, can't stand to place their lips on a dying man's mouth. Or even bang on a chest. So long as there are no outsiders present, he's a dead man."

The squeaking commode seat was accompanied by a man's voice saying, "The President's lips are in a fixed pucker, so it would be easy to breathe into his lungs."

Callins spoke, "You're not gonna catch me kissin' on his lips, with him doin' all that kissin' on a porno star's mouth."

The gravelly voice that Wilson recognized as Skip Church said, sharply, "He never did that. The press just made that story up. Now let's get back to the point. Can you get the suck sin drug?"

"That's Sucksina Coleye, and yes, I have it already."

"Is it traceable?"

"A definite 'no'." Danny Dapper tapped his head with his finger. "I've watched The President so much, I've gotten smart."

"Smart?"

"Well, my girlfriend had a nose job last week."

"Does your wife, Janet, know 'bout the nose?"

"Of course not."

"You pay for it?"

"Yep."

The woman said softly, "Janet brags about her frugality and how she manages your bank account and knows where every dollar goes."

"Well, she won't see that one, 'cause I added that cost to the expense of my recent trip to Tahiti."

"Our government has interests in Tahiti?"

"No, but the accounting office ignores this, just as they ignored your trip to the Galapagos Islands."

"No, the World Conservation Commission paid me to give a report on the administration of the policies that protect wildlife there."

"How did you get your five kids and mother-in-law paid to go with you and your wife? I'll bet you let your kids write that report," the woman said.

Dapper cleared his throat, ignored the question, and continued in his quiet diction. "I insisted that I watch the procedure in the plastic surgeon's office. I stood at the head of the operating table to observe the nose job and watched what the nurse anesthetist did. I saw her inject the stuff in her IV and place a tube in her lungs. When the nurse anesthetist was occupied placing the anesthesia tube in my girlfriend's throat, I pocketed two syringes pre-filled with Sucksina Coleye."

The gravelly voice spoke. "You'll have no trouble getting close to The President. Your seat is adjacent to his in the Cabinet Room. But how will you do it? Have him drop his pants while you stick his butt?"

"No, only doctors do that. I'll just move my arm close to him and inject a vial in his arm, through his coat sleeve. He'll be dead before he can say 'ouch'."

"But pushing a needle through his coat and dress shirt will pick up germs. That might hurt him."

"Germs won't hurt a dead man."

"Oh, right."

The squeaking of the commode was followed by, "Can you pull it off?"

The quiet voice, obviously that of Danny Dapper, replied, "You forget, I worked with a veterinarian the summer after my first year in law school."

"So, you're good at poking needles in mule butts."

"In an ass, you mean."

Callins countered. "Don't use that word."

"Shhh!"

The commode top creaked as a man let out a belly laugh. "Then let's go for the heart attack."

"I'm glad you approve. It's foolproof. The drug can't be discovered on any autopsy test, except a biopsy at the site I inject it, and they won't possibly be able to find that. I'll do it."

"When?" Harry asked.

"Next time he has a full cabinet meeting. I'll be seated directly to the left of him, and he's always leaning on me. When he's laid up against me, *Pop!* I'll stick him."

"One problem, though. It might be two months before he calls another such cabinet meeting. He hates cabinet meetings because that interferes with his watching the morning FAXY News stories."

"He watches TV all morning? Even after the FAXY buttheads started jerking his chain?"

"I dunno. Maybe he's watching cartoons now."

"That's as intelligent as the news these days."

"How does he do any work?"

"He makes all his policy decisions on the golf course or in the White House when he's playing video games."

"Ok, now I understand the late night tweets. Do we all agree that The Deed must be done?"

"I guess it's better to subjugate him in two months than never to do it at all. I'm a yes vote."

"I agree."

"Me too."

"I'm in, as well, so it's unanimous. We're going with the 'suck sin' stuff."

Because they were speaking so quietly, Wilson recognized some of the voices, but not all of them. The man to inject The President with the medical drug had a quiet voice that he thought was that of Dapper, but he wasn't one hundred percent sure. His heart pounded in his chest as he realized that all these people who were sneaking around Capitol Hill, some Democrats and some Republicans, weren't just griping or wanting to wound The President; they were actually making plans to eliminate him. He took his handkerchief and wiped his brow. *I must alert The President.*

Chapter 16

5:30 am the next morning. The Oval Office

Wilson's hands shook as he placed the Diet Coke on the Resolute desk. He spoke to The President, who was busy on Twitter. "M . . . Mr. President, there's, uh, something I'd like to tell you."

Without looking up, the leader of the country said, "Will Thompson, a happy good morning to you."

Wilson tensed his muscles to stop his shaking before beginning the carefully rehearsed speech. "Mr. P . . . President, you, uh, need to know of observations I . . . I've recently made about several of your colleagues. I, uh, fear they may be trying to harm you."

The President looked Wilson in the eyes. "Will Thompson, you're witnessing one of the finest moments in American history. I'm about to close the entire Mexican border as we all await the construction of The Great Wall of America. I'll close it down. Completely. By stopping all traffic crossings at the the border stations, and by placing two hundred thousand Army and Coast Guard service people all along the border from Brownsville, Texas to San Diego, California. That's a total distance of 1553 miles and blocks all immigration across our southern border of Texas, New Mexico, Arizona, and California. That will solve all our immigration problems. Without the Columbians, the Ecuadorians, the Venezuelans, and the Mexicans crossing into America willy nilly, our nation can save millions, no, *billions* of dollars by not having to process the *millions* of foreigners who come into America *every day*. Most of them are gang members, dope pushers, extortioners, murderers, thieves, human traffickers . . . and did I say gang members?"

"Yes, uh . . . you said that, but what about the families that just want a better place to live, where it's safe and they can make, um, a living wage?"

"A living wage? Is that what you are calling the billions and billions of welfare dollars we'd have to pay the illegals every year they're in this country?"

Wilson cringed. "Aren't, uh, you exaggerating the dollar amount?"

The President ignored the question as he was busy completing the tweet. He dramatically raised his finger to eye level and slowly dropped it and gritted as he shoved in the key to send the message. He looked up with a smile. “Oh, how I wish a camera person had filmed this grand moment so the world could see my brilliant declaration being sent around the world. Now all trade with Mexico and Central America will cease, along with all the problems that brings. And it won’t hurt our economy in the least bit. In fact, the economy will rocket sky high because this eliminates all the unpleasant and unlawful residual of NAFTA, the trade treaty that sent all our factories into Mexico. I’ll leave our military force in place until my Great Wall of America is built all the way across America’s southern border. Your President's popularity will now jump through the roof. Those that promoted NAFTA should rot in jail. Now, what was it you were saying about your observations of my colleagues? Whatever praise they heaped on me will double after they learn I've closed that border.”

“No, sir. It was about plots I've, uh, discovered to, um, inject you with . . .”

“Oh yes, I'm ahead of you on that. There's some psychiatrist wants to give me a shot of something taken from jellyfish to improve my brain function. This guy's a nut case. He states I have experienced 'cognitive decline' in making boastful statements, so he says, and he lowballs my net worth. Everyone knows that only a financial neophyte would lie about me like that. I need to write my biography so he can see all my major accomplishments in just two years in office. He'd brag, too, if he did all of the brilliant transactions as I do.”

“No, No, Mr. President. This is more serious than . . .”

“My Dad used to say, 'There's nothing more serious than a heart attack,' and he's right.”

Not only Wilson’s hands but his entire body was now shaking. He stiffened his muscles to stop the shaking, but that didn’t help. He finally blurted out, “Th . . . That's it! That's it! Let me fill you in!”

“But I know all that already.” The President looked at his computer. “Wait. There's a response to my Executive Order.”

For two minutes, The President read and re-read the first sentence of the tweet. He looked up, frowned, stared Wilson in the eyes, then finally said, slowly, "There are five responses to my tweet. The first one is . . ." He looked to the message and read, "Closure of the border will totally eliminate *all* Mexican avocados from American markets."

He prolonged his look at Wilson, then scratched his chin before turning his attention to the computer and tweeting, "That's good. We'll use only avocados grown in California."

The Twitter response was quick, with most comments along the lines of, "There are so few avocados grown in California, the stock will be gone in weeks. Plus, California avocados grow only two months a year, with one harvest. In Mexico, they grow and harvest all year long with an unlimited supply for the world market."

The President looked again at Wilson, this time through slitted eyes, for a full minute before saying, "I do like guacamole. I eat it every day, either on on my fried chicken or as a dip for my French fries. It's healthy and keeps me sharp."

Wilson stood rigidly, not blinking, breathing quite shallowly, waiting for The President to do something. *Anything would be better than him staring me down.*

Wilson sighed with relief as The President finally looked at the computer and made his Twitter response. “Then cancel the order for closing the Mexican border. Why did my advisers make such a stupid declaration without consulting me?”

He shut down the computer as Wilson asked him, “What are the other four reasons your responder gave you for cancelling your 'Close the Border' dictum?”

“Oh, I didn't bother to read them. They couldn't have been so important.” The President took a long sip of his Diet Coke, then motioned Wilson to the door.

Wilson stood in silence with a dropped jaw, trying to decide whether to laugh or scream as The President moved to Wilson’s side and pushed him into the hallway.

Chapter 17

Evening the same day. Wilson's mother's home in North Bethesda, Maryland

Wilson was a nervous wreck. *People are plotting to kill The President, but he wouldn't listen to anything I had to say. Should I be vocal? Or be quiet and let happen what would happen. After all, the Secret Service officers are always with him to keep him safe.* He had to pay a visit to his mother. She could give him advice as to how to handle this problem.

After calling Uber, he was soon on the way to her home in North Bethesda, a house he'd bought when his salary skyrocketed to $57,200 per year with his current job on Capitol Hill.

The Uber ride drove past multitudes of million-dollar homes and high-rise apartment buildings until turning at a strip shopping center and onto a two-lane road leading to a row of fifty, one-story, brick ranchers, all with well-maintained lawns and flower gardens. He felt pride as he left the Uber and walked up the brick walkway to the attractive home he'd bought with his own money: a down payment of $25,000 and a monthly payment of $1200.

He knocked once before the door was thrown open and a trim, attractively dressed woman gave him a firm and lengthy hug. He walked in to see his inexpensively decorated, roomy, 2200-square-foot house. His mom and six siblings, aged ten to eighteen, slept in the three bedrooms; the four boys were in one, with a bunk bed on each of the short walls, four individual desks along one of the long walls, and a large picture window in the other long wall that overlooked a garden busy with many colorful, blooming flowers. Even though clothes were draped over two chairs and three socks scattered over the carpet, the boys were much neater than he had been in the Virginia home in which he'd grown up. The two girls, in a smaller bedroom, slept in single beds. Between the bedrooms was a bathroom, with globs of toothpaste and strings of dental floss strewn on the black and white, checkerboard-tiled floor. Wilson's mother had a room to herself with a private bath. He didn't venture there.

"Mom, I like the way everything is so neat and clean. You could eat from the floor."

"Well, we've been here two years and sometimes it is. But kids are kids, and it's not always like a fairy princess' castle. But we're all happy, and appreciative of your letting us be in this beautiful home. It's in a good school district with doctors' and lawyers' kids sitting alongside mine. And they're all doing good, with Matthew being at the top of his class and all the kids making A's and B's. There's plenty of room here for you, and we'd love to have you live with us."

Wilson thought about the tiny garage apartment he was renting in DC with one room and a bathroom and shower. "No, Mom. I'm fine. Just fine. I need to be close to my work until I get enough money to buy a car. And I'm so pleased how you fixed this up so nicely."

His mother poured coffee and brought out cookies she'd made yesterday. "I know you have something you need to tell me."

"Why do you say that?"

“Because I'm your Mom, and whenever you come to me with a look like that on your face, I know something’s bothering you and you want my advice.”

They sat and sipped coffee for several minutes before he opened up and told her of the conversations he'd overheard concerning the presumed threat to The President and The President's refusal to listen to his warning. “Mom, what should I do? I can't afford to lose my job, like all other whistleblowers in government jobs. And there's no other job I can take with my lack of education that pays what I need to support this family and this house.”

His mother frowned briefly before smiling. “Thomas, you must always do what's right. That's the most important thing.”

“But you and the kids are my greatest concern.”

She shook her head. “No. No matter what, we'll be alright. I have the part-time job in a lawyer's office and can take up the slack if you have to work at a lesser-paying job, such as you had working for the senator in Bethesda. And Jamey is a senior in high school. But remember. The people that are harshly judging The President are doing so on their own initiatives. The President hasn't been convicted of any wrongdoing. Maybe he's stumbling, just like you did for so long."

"But Jamey is a smart kid. He must go to college. I'll work day and night if it needs to be. I won't allow him to stop his schooling until he has a bachelor's degree . . . or better," he mumbled.

His mother reached and placed her hand on his cheek. "If you let Our President die when you could have stopped it, even if he were to be proven a wicked man, that will burden your conscience the rest of your life, and mine as well. Always do what is right, no matter what the penalty."

"How will I know what is right?"

"Right may be one thing in one situation and something else in another. And I know you. You'll choose properly."

"But I'm just a small person in his eyes. He's used to listening to advice from important advisors and world leaders, and even with that, he pays absolutely no attention to what *they* say. Why would he listen to me?"

She shook her head and looked deeply into his eyes. “That's sometimes difficult. I've been your mother for twenty-five years. I've seen you take control of the kids as they came along. When you heaped all the Christmas presents on them when your salary jumped up after you were hired by the senator, you gave them so many toys, they didn't know which to play with. You quickly directed them to the educational toys, the ones that will help them grow and develop their minds. Just like The President. He's had so many toys with his billions of dollars, he doesn't know with which to play. The Presidency seems to be just a game with him, and I'm betting you can direct him to what's important, just like you did for your brothers and sisters.”

“But Mom, The President’s a grown man. Why is he going to take my advice when he won't even listen to that given by his advisers, some of the smartest people in the world? If I do as you say, he'll fire me on the spot like he's done to other important people when they say things he doesn’t want to hear.”

His mother squinted and scratched her nose. “You remember how your Dad used to whip you for even minor infractions?”

“I remember he beat me a lot, but I also recall that every time he did so, you showered me with so many kisses and big chunks of homemade apple pie . . .”

“With ice cream.”

“Yes, and you were so good to me after the whippings, it made me glad to be whipped, just for what you always did afterward.”

“You have it, my boy. But in this situation, you must be your Mama and your Papa.”

“You mean, I must whip up on him to make him change, but then, 'nice him' so much, he doesn't even realize he's taken a whipping?”

“That's exactly right. You have a way about you, like with the kids, and The President is just a grown-up kid. You can handle him. And nobody on this earth can do it like you.”

Chapter 18

8 pm the next day.
The Georgetown home of Deuce Hardway

Deuce Hardway excused himself from the dinner table in the Georgetown section of DC. The Democratic congressman said he had an appointment with the vice president at the White House. While his wife cleared the kitchen, he quietly went to his dressing room. Hardway was a trim, fit man with salt and pepper hair, a distinct widow's peak, and a clean-shaven face. He removed his starched, white shirt and black tie and put on a crumpled, long-sleeved, denim shirt. Hardway slipped into a brown Harris Tweed sport coat, pulled the collar over his neck, and quietly left the house carrying a large shopping bag from Neiman Markups.

He hailed a taxi outside his home and instructed the cabbie to drop him off at the convenience store next to the Manly's Hardware. In the cab, he removed from his sack a wide-brimmed, Indy Jones hat. He put it on, then ducked his head from the cabbie's view and used a small mirror to stick in place a large, black, brushy mustache. Lastly, he added a pair of wide, black-framed sunglasses while keeping hidden behind the seat.

On reaching his destination, he placed a $50 bill in the driver's hand, without exposing his face, and slipped out the door. He kept his back to the cab until it was well out of sight, then removed and stuffed his sport coat in his brown paper bag. He looked at his reflection in the hardware store window, pulled the brim of his hat lower to his eyebrows, then scrutinized his image. After a minute, he smiled. "Perfect," he said, as he walked into the store.

He looked at the floor and walked to the key maker in the rear of the store, keeping his head down. The brim of the hat concealed his view of the five-foot-tall, vertical rack of fifty blank keys.

WHAM! He walked into it, scattering keys over a wide swath of floor. Still keeping his head low, with his face out of sight, he grabbed handfuls of the blank keys and stood, placing a lot of them on the counter while kicking the others underneath.

The keymaker continued cutting a key, paying no attention to the commotion, until his clumsy customer spoke to him. “Sir.”

“Yes?”

Hardway lifted his head briefly to see the thin, white-haired man with heavily tanned skin look at him with a serious expression. “Are you Carlos?” he asked.

“Yes, sir.”

“I'm Bob Jones. You don't know me, but I met Reyna Santos yesterday. She says you have some special rat toy I can buy.”

Carlos squinted his eyes as he studied the customer, then smiled. “Yes, yes. She told me, and I brought some today. Are your rats . . . big ones?”

Lowering his chin to his chest, Hardway responded, “Actually they're wolves. A half dozen come to my home out in the country. I need a large dose.”

“Ahh,” he said in a now quiet voice. “Now I know exactly what you want.” He looked from side to side and lowered his voice. “Do you have the thousand bucks?”

Hardway palmed the money that was tightly folded into a wad and placed it in Carlos' hand.

"Here's your key," Carlos spoke loudly, as he dropped a blank key in a bag already containing a cigarette-sized package and passed it.

He looked at the package, then at the man. "Tell me about how to use it?"

"Of course. This is a benzo-dia-tria-napa-papa-mama-pria-zipperine. It's a concentrated powder that's absolutely tasteless. They call this 'goofballs' on the street. It's like unadulterated water. You can put your finger in a glass of it and put a drop on your tongue. You'll see. No taste at all. Try it. He smiled as he said, with his voice raised, "The formula is my own. I make it myself. A spoonful will knock a guy — a wolf — on his can, and two spoonfuls will knock him deader-na door nail. Two spoons of it in a glass of water *will not* be tasted, and he — the man, the wolf — will never know. Ten minutes and the man — wolf — is history."

The buyer half smiled and turned to walk away.

"Nice doing business with you, Senator Hardway," Carlos said.

The purchaser stiffened. Bizarre contortions twisted his face, separating the left side of the mustache from his upper lip, leaving one side of it falling over his mouth. His eyes were completely round as he ran from the store, smacking a stand of sunglasses near the door and scattering them all over the storefront.

Chapter 19

8:30 pm a week later.
Hardway's Hotel Hilldrop Hideaway office

Deuce Hardway felt nervous as he looked at the three men and one woman standing around the writing table in his two-room, luxury suite. He wondered how it would be possible to resolve an issue in a bipartisan manner in Washington, where it was difficult to reach a decision on *anything*. But here was such a group: Democrats that wanted a Republican president removed and Republicans who wanted their own party's president taken out of office in such a manner as to prevent negative feedback against the Republican Party. He felt pride in "doing" this as a "miracle," seeing it was the last straw to save the country.

Hardway's purpose in today's secret gathering was to demonstrate his purchased poison to the group of his assassination associates. As they awaited the arrival of the final member of their group, Republican Jonas

Hopalong, Hardway filled a hotel glass with Deja Red mineral water and spooned in a measured quantity of his purchase.

"Shouldn't we put in two cubes of ice?"

"This place is such a dump; I'd be afraid the ice may be poisoned."

"Hmmm."

They turned on the lights to see if the water-poison mixture could be detected by any discoloration. It was perfectly clear.

"Let's try a taste test."

"You taste it. It's your idea."

"If you kick off, whom should we get to take your place on the transportation committee?"

Hardway smiled as he dipped his forefinger in the water and touched his tongue, then smacked his lips a couple times before saying, "Tastes like water to me. No kick at all."

One said, "I'll take your word for it," as another dipped his finger in the glass, touched his tongue and smiled. "You're right, but how are we going to get this in water that The President will drink?"

Just then, Jonas Hopalong, the delinquent member of the group, burst into the room clutching his chest and popping a nitroglycerine tablet in his mouth. "I need water," he said, as he grabbed the demonstration glass in both hands, shoved it to his mouth, then chugged every drop.

The group stood, stiff and paralyzed, for a second.

Then, Hardway shoved the remaining poison in his pocket and ran out the door screaming, "Call the EMT's on 911! Call the EMT's!"

"What shall I tell them?"

"That the dead man overdosed on some dope named benzo-dia-triasomething!"

The *Unposted*'s headline the next day read: HOPALONG PASSES ALONG-GOOFBALL GOOF-UP. FOUL PLAY PLOY PERHAPS. Wilson paused a moment after reading it. *Could this "mistake" actually be another Republican with intentions of harming The President?*

Chapter 20

Evening two days later.
The Capitol Hill office of Hollie Mackril

Hollie hovered over her computer for several hours studying a book, *The Zombie Game*, written by a medical doctor. Next, she searched the internet and found another book, *Rainbows Emanating From Serpents*, by an anthropologist who had studied Zombies and written extensively about their behavior and how it was controlled. She read over and over a passage telling how real Zombies were still being created in Haiti, scribbling notes about the chemicals the two authors proposed, then probed even deeper in the internet, tracing these chemicals until her watch indicated the time: 10:50 pm. Mackril knew she needed to hurry to make her important meeting. She half ran, half jogged to the Abner Apartment Building on Tenth Street, a structure that had been abandoned and uninhabited for three years. A light flashed for a split second in the otherwise totally darkened building. She approached a side door which had a broken padlock beneath a "Condemned Building" sign. She entered, opened the creaking door of room 44, and faced her four co-conspirators, all Republicans, waiting in the hallway by room 44. A single candle provided illumination.

"Any success?"

Her eyes sparkled as she said, "Yes. And you will all like this. I know that, like myself, none of you really want to hurt The President. Our desire is to change his actions in order to save our Democracy. I have a plan that meets both of these criteria."

Several sighs were emitted from the group.

"I propose we make him the first Zombie President."

"Yuck. I don't want to be around a dead person with rotting flesh and bones sticking out all over him. That makes me sick. Let's just shoot him."

A man spoke quickly. "No, no. A shooting will bring a huge investigation, and we'll all get caught and thrown in jail."

The new arrival threw her shoulders back and spoke with a confident air. "No, no. There's no rotting flesh or exposed bones sticking out of real Zombies. The tradition was transferred from West Africa when enslaved farm laborers were transported to Haiti in the seventeenth century. In 1850, a self-governing group of slave workers was formed to maintain discipline among their peers. Creation of Zombies was the harshest form of punishment meted out by the group. Those convicted of crimes by their leaders were punished by being given drugs that subdued the criminals' frontal lobes."

"Like the pre-frontal lobotomies described in the movie, *Few Flew Over the Cuckoo Cuckold*?"

"Not at all. That required surgery, which was irreversible. This involves altering one's mental state with drugs which can be dosage controlled and reversed at any time."

"That's not the way it is in the *Night After the Morning of the Afternoon of Living Dead*."

Senator Dick Dingledorf spoke. "The Hollywood portrayal is not the way Zombies are in real life. They look just like all of us but are subservient when given orders and suggestions by others. They're real people but with their frontal lobes subdued by drugs."

"It would sure be nice if The President would just choose to do what we recommend once in a while. He rarely asks our opinion, and even when we give it, he always twitters a mandate on everything that *he* thinks should be done, even if we all oppose it. If we don't get him to listen to us . . ."

"I like that. I like that. But how do we buy the drugs without getting caught?"

"It's not a drug. It's a weed, Jimson weed. It grows wild and is common in Virginia."

"Yeah, I know about Jimson weed. I have a farm in Middleburg, Virginia, and that weed grows everywhere we don't mow the grass for a couple months. My farm manager is afraid it will make our horses sick, so he's always on the lookout for it. I can have him cut a bunch for us."

"What kind of sick?"

"It's a psychedelic thing. They go temporarily loco. Crazy in the head."

"What's that have to do with our problem?"

"It makes anyone subservient to the wishes of others. They take it and, like the Haitian slaves of the 1800's, follow the orders of others. Zombies look the same as real people and act the same but have no ability to dominate. Or ignore what we say."

"Like he does us."

"Yes. We'll make the decisions, and he will follow our orders by giving others the orders we want implemented. Plus, he'll be a nice guy for the first time in his life. People will like him for being cooperative. It's a total win-win."

"I like it," was the response of one and echoed by the four others.

"What kind of poison is it?"

"It's not so much a poison as it contains drugs medical doctors use — Atropine and Scopolamine. As such, we can control it to keep from killing him and reverse it if we don't like the effects of it or if he changes to the point of his not needing it anymore."

"That'll be a cold day in Hell, for him to change anything at all about himself."

"Does the weed have a poisonous seed?"

"No. The entire plant — the roots, leaves, the flowering blooms, and seed — all contain the drug."

"That's good, but how do we get the weed in The President?"

"That's our real problem. He's always been afraid of being poisoned. He'll never eat in a local restaurant, only in national franchises. That eliminates one possibility. The other problem is that he eats primarily fast food burgers, fries, and pizzas — except for the crust."

"How can you eat a pizza and leave the crust?"

"I guess you'd have to lick the sauce, cheese, and pepperonis off the crust first."

"I'm sure even porno stars won't kiss him after pizza. Whew. It makes my breath so bad that I use mouthwash before getting anywhere near my girlfriend."

"For dinner, the White House staff often cook him a large T-bone steak that's not just well-done, but cooked til it's burned to a crisp."

"Double yuck."

"It sounds perfectly awful, but that's how he likes steak."

"What's he do for breakfast?"

"Doesn't go for breakfast."

"And we all know he only drinks Diet Coke."

“Then how do we cross that hurdle? Getting him to ingest the Jimson weed?”

“I have an idea. We’ll intercept the steak the White House cook prepares for him and sprinkle a powder of Jimson weed on it. With his burned steak, he’ll never even taste it. Once we get it into him, he’ll never object to our even overtly making him eat the stuff.”

“Yes. And then maintain the medication with tea made from the leaves of the plant.”

“How do we know how much to feed him without killing him?”

Dingledorf waved his hand and stood. “My wife has a dog and her brother is a pharmacist. Both she and her brother support actions we are discussing tonight.”

“’What’s your wife, a pharmacist, and a dog have anything to do with all this?”

Dingledorf answered, “Her dog is a Great Dane named Oscar. He weighs 190 pounds. That's close to the weight of The President, who is only thirty or forty pounds heavier. Let’s get my brother-in-law, the pharmacist, to feed it to Oscar til he starts to get sick, then back off that amount.”

"What if it kills the dog?"

"That'll be a bonus. I hate that dog. He sleeps at night between me and my wife. She loves him so much, she doesn't want me to even touch her anymore."

"He doesn't . . ."

"No, no, no. I sure wish he did. That would take care one of my big problems. Those Viagra pills are really expensive."

Hollie Mackril's soft voice piped in. "Enough of that. You're implying that your wife and the dog have some sort of emotional attachment — or even worse. You're making me blush."

Another said, "So, we get The President under our control with Jimson weed. Then what do we do?"

Boomer Blaster's booming voice answered. "We'll keep him close to us and direct his actions to be more rational and be a strong voice for his political advisors and our constituents."

"But his wife will know."

"She won't miss him. She spends most of her time away from him."

"Does she have a dog too?" the quiet voice asked.

Chapter 21

10 am three weeks later. The Cabinet Room

The cabinet members were all there, less the secretaries of interior and energy, who had been fired by The President within the last few weeks; Hardy Workman, labor secretary, who was asked to leave the cabinet while The President decided whether to terminate him or promote him to Veterans Affairs; and Badly Buster Badcock, who was under consideration for secretary of state if the current acting secretary of state would transfer to budget director and the acting budget position transferred to labor. Also empty was the seat of the domestic affairs secretary, Godfry Damhim, who was awaiting presidential pardon for his capital murder conviction for the axe mutilation of his wife and her six brothers.

Sipping on a Diet Coke, The President was seated, looking at the cover of the recent *Rocking Rock Stars* magazine that bore his picture. His back was to a window overlooking the White House Rose Garden. Danny

Dapper, the secretary of defense, stood to the left of The President and fidgeted with an object in his coat pocket as he looked nervously at The President.

The President clapped his hands once, and everyone — in unison — rolled back their cushy, padded desk chairs, seated themselves, and positioned their legs under the table, then folded their hands atop the table. Dapper looked across the table, to the right of the Vice President Pennypincher, into the staring eyes of Harry Johns, the secretary of transportation. Johns grimaced as he momentarily put his hand on his painful left knee, rubbed it, and then jumped when The President spoke to him. "Harry, are your knees any better?"

Harry John's eyes darted to those of The President. "Thank you for asking, sir. And thank you for giving me those arthritis pills last week. I haven't had any pain. You are truly a miracle worker, and in addition to all the other great things you do, you're a marvelous doctor."

The President smiled broadly and spread his arms to his audience saying, "Did all of you hear that? My own cabinet secretary praises my diagnosing arthritis of his knees. And I cured him with a medicine I ordered from

Amwayzon, just for him. Be sure CNS hears about that. I solve not only world problems but also medical problems of my own staff."

Veep Pennypincher began an applause that quickly spread around the table like a line of dominoes.

The President smacked his hands together once, and the clapping immediately ceased. "We must proceed. You all know my extremely busy schedule that begins at 5:30 am each morning and doesn't end until 1 am, so today we'll limit our business to three problems for discussion. What's first?"

Harry Johns raised his hand, but The President recognized Mary Spender, the acting budget director. Spender frowned. "Mr. President, your tax legislation initially boosted our economy. People thought they had more money and spent it all until the tariffs against the Chinese raised the price of goods so high, their yearn for yen bottomed out, leaving no pot to pay on. This chart shows that."

She held up a 3x5-foot section of paperboard and pointed at the four lines printed in letters large enough to be read the length of a football field away. Spender gave a wordy explanation of the brief summary as depicted on the chart: "Point one. Retail spending initially increased fifteen percent, then dropped to four percent before jumping back up to nine percent, which is a fraction behind what we saw in quarter two, where an initial seven percent jumped to eleven percent before bottoming out at three." She dropped her finger to the second line. "Our Gross Domestic Product jumped a huge one point four percent in the first week of the quarter before equalizing with the fourth quarter of the previous year, which was a record for imported goods in an odd year. Does everybody understand?" No hands were raised, but all eyebrows shot up.

The President, after two minutes of letting all this information soak in his head, nodded. "Yes. That's a good report. It shows all the good my policies have generated. Please go on."

Moving to the third line, Spender read, "Our exports of American-made cars jumped three point one percent. That's slightly behind the Korean autos that climbed to a weak twenty-five percent."

"Terrific. That's twenty-eight point one percent."

Slowly, she read the fourth line: "Textile production is up one point two percent, but costs doubled, limiting the tangible resource allocation to one-fifth; of course, that's with rounding the numbers to five decimal points and subtracting the lesser of the divisors to a dividend-equality analysis of a quarter less a four percent quotient for expendable goods, which leaves a six percent loss in tangible profits."

The President studied the chart for a full five minutes while all the cabinet members squirmed in their seats. Finally, he smiled and patted his own shoulder. "That's the best economic news this country has ever had, going back to 1900. No President has been able to show such a leap in economic growth as this. Not ever in the history of our nation, or any other nation in this world. I told everyone while I campaigned for this office that I would be the greatest leader this country has ever had. And in only two years, I have done what no other President has ever been able to do."

Everyone at the table clapped softly. He stood, and the intensity of the applause increased. Danny Dapper looked around at his associates, who seemed to feel obligated to clap as long as The President stood. He looked at the watch on his arm and saw five minutes pass before The President finally sat. The clapping abruptly ceased.

"Who will have our second point of discussion?"

Dapper looked across the table as Harry Johns raised his hand and waved it, determined to be one of the next two cabinet members to be heard today.

The President looked to his right and recognized the agriculture secretary.

Secretary Diggins held up a section of paperboard that looked exactly like that of his predecessor. "Mr. President, I also have a . . ." he dropped his voice as he said, "good report to present."

He read the first line of the chart, printed by the same printer the others used. "Corn and soybean production have improved eight percent since you took office."

The President placed his hand on his chin and studied the large letters of that first line. For five minutes. Then he nodded his head. "Good. That's good. Next point."

"Point two: Agricultural exports are up six percent."

The President did his math with his treaty-signing pen and followed, "Yes, that's fifteen percent."

"Fourteen percent, sir."

"Yes, that's what I said, didn't I?"

"And imports are at an all-time high of thirty percent."

He wrote figures on his paper before concluding, "Then you are reporting a forty-four percent total economic factor?"

The group began to clap before Diggins could find any words to say.

The President stood and clapped loudly, then looked at his Vice President. "Vice President Pennypincher, to what do you attribute that amazing improvement?"

"Sir, this is all due to your decisive actions with world leaders to assert our nation, as Leader of the World, to demand they reciprocate our generosity and give us our due respect."

"That all?"

A female voice, that of Bab Babs Callins, secretary of health and human services, spoke in a sing-song tone. “Mr. President, it's more than that. They know that you're serious about adding import tariffs on their goods and, quite frankly, they’re scared of you. They’re cooperating to bypass your fury.” She then turned her head slightly and looked first at Dapper, then at Johns, who shrugged his shoulders slightly.

The President folded his arms on his chest for a few minutes, then spoke. “Secretary Diggins, I congratulate you on such a clear and concise report. Be sure the media get copies of this report and that they print *this* rather than all their ‘false news’ they enjoy so much. I want our nation, even the entire world, to know what my administration is doing. Something no other president has ever done, and I've only been in office two years. That's quite remarkable, isn't it? In only two years we — I've — done all that.”

The President stared at the chart for another five minutes until Secretary Diggins asked, “Mr. President, don't you want to see my last two lines?”

The president looked at his watch, then shook his head, "No. With a report like that there's no need to go farther. Let's have one last report."

Harry Johns half-stood and waved his hand wildly. This was the last chance for maybe two months until the next cabinet meeting. He had to be recognized.

The President looked up and down the table and finally pointed across the table to his transportation secretary. "Well, Johns, you're so anxious to give your report, it must be a good one."

"Yes, sir. It's a great one." He held up his poster.

Danny Dapper slowly dropped his right hand into his pocket, snapped the syringe from its protective case and one-handedly popped the cap from the needle. Then, he transferred it to his left hand. *The Sucksina Coleye was ready for delivery*. He caught Church's eye and nodded.

Johns read the large letters of the first line as Dapper leaned toward The President.

"Intermodal transportation budget is lower than projection by twenty-five percent."

Dapper tensed as the time for the injection was near. But he needed to move two inches closer to The President to keep from being seen. He leaned ever so slightly with the syringe, ready for the kill. He took a deep breath and started to move the needle for the injection.

Suddenly, The President sat upright.

"Yes, sir?" Johns asked.

"I have a question."

"Yes?"

Dapper took a deep breath and pulled the syringe back.

"Mr. Secretary, our intermodal is doing quite well. How about the other bathroom fixtures we place on the world market?"

Johns sighed. He took a deep breath and replied, "Quite well, sir. Quite well."

"Good," The President said, as he scratched a note on a pad in front of him.

Johns looked again at Dapper and rolled his eyes. Dapper regained his poise and looked at Johns, motioning his head to the left and down.

Johns gave a slight nod, dropped the poster lower and to the right, and resumed. “The Federal Highway System was under budget. It dropped from four point two billion dollars to three point seven five.”

The President had to lean lower and closer to Dapper to see the poster after it was moved. “That's good, is it?”

“Yes, sir. We saved 450 million dollars.”

“That's really good.”

“Yes, sir. That's a lot of money for you to transfer to your military budget. That’s enough for a down payment on the new F-22.”

The President was slow to respond. Then he nodded his head twice. “Yes, yes, I'd like to do that. But in your report to the press, tell them that the money will go to bolster Medicaid. The people will like it.”

“Yes, sir.”

Johns looked at Dapper, who again nodded his head to the left and downward.

Johns gave a slight nod, twisted the chart, and lowered it to the table.

As The President shifted to the left and lowered his head to see, Dapper lifted himself slightly off his seat so he could move the needle closer . . . a little closer . . . then his arm touched The President's arm. Then Dapper closed his eyes and shoved the needle toward the target arm.

At the same moment, realization hit The President that his throat was dry, dry because he hadn't had a sip of his Diet Coke in over ten minutes. His left arm shot forward, and he grasped the Coke, just as Dapper's syringe shot past the arm rest, and came to rest on The President's lap.

The President recognized the problem immediately.

"Secretary Dapper, I didn't know you were a diabetic and needed your insulin."

A shocked Secretary Dapper nodded a defensive "Yes, sir," as The President snatched the syringe and smacked it into Dapper's gluteus maximus muscle, thereby injecting the drug. "Here. I'll save your life too."

Dapper's mouth dropped open. Callins screamed. Johns tried to speak, but Dapper was already paralyzed.

His muscles didn't respond. He couldn't breathe. Church ran to Dapper as he fell to the floor. The President dropped on his knees beside him and placed his always-puckered lips near Dapper's mouth. After hastily blowing two puffs in Dapper's direction, he abruptly turned to Church. "Keep doing what I started, for a minute or so."

Church looked at Johns and shrugged as he mouthed the words, "But I didn't take the chest massage course, either."

The President scowled as he placed his hand on Church's back and shoved his face toward that of Dapper. Church took a deep breath inches away from the downed man's face and *Whoosh!* He blew as hard as he could, showering Dapper's face with air from his lungs and thick saliva. Church stopped to look at The President who said, "Good job. Now do it a couple more times."

Church *Whoosh*ed! At Dapper's face again before The President lifted a limp Dapper to his chair, placing him in a seated position.

As The President opened his mouth to speak, Dapper's body slumped over on his side. "Oh, no. This is a crisis," he said. Callins jumped to her feet to assist her colleague, but The President held out both hands to stop her efforts, saying, "No, no. That's nice of you to try to help, but with what I did, everything's OK." He snapped his fingers. Two black-suited men rushed in.

Callins looked at Dapper, momentarily feeling relief, until the two young men ran to The President rather than Dapper. With brushes and warm cloths, they brushed and wiped the wrinkles from The President suit.

Callins and Church moved toward Dapper but were shooed away as The President said, "I assure you all, this man is quite alright. With a diabetic crisis, it takes a few minutes for the insulin to take effect."

His colleagues eyed Dapper in alarm but couldn't reveal their secret. Dapper proposed this. It failed. Now he had to accept the consequences.

Dapper remained motionless in his chair as The President asked Johns to complete his reading of the last two lines. Church's eyes flickered back and forth between The President and Dapper.

The President sat after John's presentation with his arms folded across his chest, his posture tall and rigid, and looked into John's eyes a full five minutes before speaking. "Tell the press that Secretary Dapper had a diabetic crisis, and I gave him his insulin, then administered cardiopulmonary resuscitation and brought him back. Tell them I'm a hero for all that, but do . . . not . . . report . . . anything else . . . until . . . tomorrow."

Callins stood slowly and walked quietly behind The President.

The President was aware of her actions but pretended not to see her.

Callins lifted Dapper's arm and felt for the pulse, then raised one of his closed eyelids. Tears came to her eyes as she whispered, "He's really dead."

The President looked at Callins as he said, "Then take the brass nameplate from the back of his chair and send it to his widow." He snapped his fingers, and one of The President's aides came in, grabbed Dapper's ankles, and dragged him away. The meeting was dismissed. Callins and Church remained wide-eyed in their positions as the others left the room.

Wilson read the next day's *Unposted* headlines: PRESIDENT DODGES DAPPER DEATH. The text of the article continued, "Butt stick stuck, Defense Dapper downed in diabetic disaster. Recovery from doctors deemed death-dodging doubtful. Members of his cabinet lauded The President's actions, which prolonged the Dapper life, giving him another day."

Wilson shivered at the thought that Dapper must have made a mistake trying to use the drug he talked about in the bathroom meeting with Callins and Johns. *I feel sorry for him, but he was trying to kill The President. Does anybody else know about this but me? I must do something to keep anyone from succeeding where Dapper and others have failed.*

Chapter 22

Midnight one week later. Dingledorf's pharmacist brother-in-law's garage laboratory next door to Wall Market in the Greenaway shopping district of Greater Foggy Bottom

The preparations were complete. The pharmacist ground the Jimson weed into a powder after drying the seeds of all moisture, mixed it with traditional steak seasoning granules, and fed it to his sister and brother-in-law's Great Dane as the senator and his wife spent the day at Greenaway's Foggy Bottom Spa. The first feeding of the big dog was on a piece of raw steak. But the dog surprised the pharmacist by licking the Jimson weed preparation from the meat. He liked it better than the steak! That made it easy. Using a Veterinarian's heart monitor and blood pressure cuff, and backed up with an EKG machine and defibrillator, he slowly fed the dog his preparation. He titrated the drug against the pulse and blood pressure. He added the drug until the dog's pulse began to drop and the blood pressure started to lower. That was it. With the dog-to-President weight ratio being seventy-six to one hundred, the proper dosage was calculated.

Chapter 23

11 pm. Abner Apartment Building, Room 44

The pharmacist huddled with Mackril and the Republican senators as he described his pleasure with his drug creation. He detailed his research and was jubilant as he projected the probability of success with his Zombie preparation. They had numerous questions for which, with his knowledge of Jimson weed gathered from an extensive review of available texts, he gave answers that quieted the fears of each member of the group.

A vote was taken: All five agreed to proceed with the project. The big question remained: How were they going to get The President to ingest it? Someone close to The President had to administer the drug. The consensus was that the only outsider The President seemed to trust was one who enjoyed frequent contact with him, someone who regularly questioned — even to The President's face — some of his erratic decisions, and he still hadn't been fired: Thomas Wilson.

But would Wilson be willing to do this, especially given the risks? It wasn't assassination, though there could be huge repercussions. And if he was in opposition to the idea, more of a loyalist to The President than country, would he report the group to law enforcement? This was clearly a violation of the law, not just to administer the drug but also just to plan such an act. And to instruct another individual to give a toxic substance was as much a violation as the act of giving it oneself. All of those present knew the consequences of what they were doing and voted to limit their liability to one person, one that could be trusted not to expose the others if they were wrong about Wilson. In lieu of taking an odd-man out choice, Wilson's friend Hollie Mackril volunteered. She sent by courier a message to Wilson: "Meet me for a confidential discussion in the Abner Apartments, room 44, tomorrow at 11 pm."

Chapter 24

11:20 pm that evening.
Wilson's office in The Capitol Building

The invitation frightened Wilson, given all that he'd heard and seen about what others had attempted and failed at doing. *Why does Hollie want to meet me and why so late at night? She's never asked me to meet her outside of our lunch meetings. Could she be a part of another scheme to harm The President? Why would she want to involve me? She knows I'm loyal to him and wouldn't want to hurt him. And if she does want to involve me, I know the punishment would be severe and I can't do that to my family. My family . . . Maybe I should go see mom and get her advice.*

Feeling incredibly anxious about what might be asked of him, and not trusting the security of the telephone system, even with the so-called "secrecy apps," he called Uber.

Midnight the same day.
Wilson's mother's house in North Bethesda

Wilson's mother didn't seem surprised to see him. She greeted him with a warm hug, as always, and invited him in while his six siblings slept, as if they had planned the visit ages ago. She listened to his story, which was accurate in describing the invitation and the plots he knew about against The President but deficient in naming individuals. From his observations of the clandestine activities of those trying to dispose of The President, he told her of his fear that he was going to be asked to assist in some way with one of the plots. He described his cordial relationship with the sender of the note and that the only reason he considered acceptance of the invitation was the good-hearted nature of his friend. She was one to be trusted and not feared. She could never do anything to hurt Wilson, and though he recognized that there were problems with The President that needed attention, he was concerned people seemed to think that killing him was the only answer.

His mother's concluding statements were not unexpected. "There's no harm in hearing what she has to say just to be sure that's indeed what she's asking of you. Decide what's best for America first. Then let everything else fall into its place. If you quit or lose your job, we as a family can continue. I will work full-time, and Jamey can take a job and do his college online."

Wilson shook his head. "No. I don't want that. If I just stay quiet about all this, life will continue as it is now. With no sacrifices for you and the kids and a comfortable life for me."

"If you stay quiet without even hearing what she is proposing and something happens — whether to the country because of The President, or even to The President which you might have helped stop — will that be a burden for your conscience to bear for the rest of your life? She must be consulting you because she, as I do, sees your ability to make decisions with careful thought and integrity."

"But I'll manage. I always do. But I couldn't live with knowing I've sacrificed the family's well-being."

"Hush, hush. We've already talked about it, and it will be just fine no matter what. Jamey's well-motivated and can get the online bachelor's degree and a good job after that."

"But, what if I . . ."

"If you decide to participate in an activity for which, rightly or not, they convict you of a crime? I know you. You'll make the right decision. Whatever it is you end up doing, I have no doubt you'll be a big national hero. If you find the right way to help the country, even if it's just by helping The President, who we all know by now listens to you, they'll parade with your life-sized picture. If The President is found to be as horrible as the insiders say, they can burn him in effigy. Whatever happens, you'll have our full support, and half the country's as well. But before any of that happens, just remember what I told before."

"I'll kick his ass like Dad did me . . ."

"And then praise him like a saint," she added.

Chapter 25

11 pm the next day. The Abner Apartments, Room 44

Wilson knocked lightly, then entered the room. In the light of a small candle, he saw the outline of a tall, thin woman in a black, dressy, pantsuit. As he moved closer, he saw the unmistakable face of his friend Hollie Mackril. She extended her hand as he approached.

Her high-pitched voice crackled as she began talking. "Well, you know who I am, and you will have control of my fate after I give you my proposal. I have met a lot of individuals in DC, but you're different. You're like a brother to me, and that's why I'm here today. Being a cabinet member, I'd like to say that I have input into the regulations in my department, but The President ignores all my department recommendations, as he does for most of the current cabinet members. Therefore, I — well, the entire cabinet, really — am unable to effectively do my job on behalf of the people of our nation. And the nation is suffering because of it. He has become the sole voice of the government, and as such, I feel he violates the principles of our Constitution — which we officials are charged with defending and upholding. It's the essence of *our* oath of office. And his . . ."

Wilson listened as she rattled out her long list of grievances about ways The President violated *his* oath of office, thereby obstructing everyone else's ability to protect the country, concluding with, "We must stop him. Though I know I'll lose my job, and probably my freedom, I must do something to restore normalcy to our government and save the country. I am asking you to . . ." She went on to explain the use of the Jimson weed, how it wouldn't kill him, as they didn't want him dead, but it would diminish his aggressive authoritative stranglehold he had on the nation and allow the normal pace of government to return to America and ensure the Democracy would be retained. Tears were in her eyes as she asked, "Thomas Wilson, will you work with us . . . uhh, me . . . and administer the initial dose of the medication?"

Wilson's response was, "Ms. Mackril, I know where you're coming from, but . . . I sorta like this guy. He and I hit it off pretty well now. I used to stutter around him because he's so powerful and I found that intimidating, but with his help, I think I'm getting over that. I certainly don't want anybody to even hurt him, let alone even kill . . . But I've been thinking a lot since you invited me to meet. With what you've just told me about the drug, I have an idea. Just maybe it'll work."

Secretary Mackril slowly lifted a bulky backpack and held it toward Wilson.

Wilson did not accept it without more thought, but when he, at last, took it from her hand, she sighed, gave him a big hug, then quickly departed.

Chapter 26

**Midnight the same day.
A very, very tiny office next to the Oval Office**

Wilson reviewed the contents of the backpack. There was a tape-sealed shoebox and eight pages of typed directions on the drug, its dosage, explicit directions as to the administration, the anticipated reaction of The President to the drug, and ending with the caution, "If he faints, becomes delusional or maniacal, convulses, has blurred vision, drowsiness, or becomes hostile, call 911 and see that he receives prompt medical care. No one wants him to die. Such a call for help will place you in jeopardy of prosecution, and anyone else who had a hand in planning the project as well. It's all on the line, but the promise of saving the country and restoring a democratic government is worth every risk."

It was a long night for Wilson as he weighed his options. It crossed his mind that he was being taken advantage of, using his closeness to The President to further their own personal needs and desires. He never believed

Secretary Mackril acted without the support of others in government. That was made obvious by the complexity of the proposed project. But that she was willing to take the fall alone showed just how greatly she was dedicated to it.

He re-lived his experiences with Mackril. In her continued contact with Wilson, she had become a friend; someone to eat peanut butter sandwiches with, to laugh with as the squirrels sat in front of them on the bench and begged for a piece of their sandwiches, and to just talk, sometimes concerning the popularity of political decisions but mostly about family, about friendships, about weather, how pretty the cherry blossoms were this year, the beauty of the reflective pond in the noon sunlight, and stuff. Just stuff that friends are comfortable sharing — with a friend.

No, it's not in her being to take advantage of me. She is a true patriot — with nothing personal to take from me and a willingness to sacrifice herself, like the many true patriots of American history. I trust her.

Chapter 27

5:30 am the next morning. The Oval Office

He was still mulling it over in his mind when he took the clippings and a Diet Coke to The President the next morning. His boss was unusually pensive when Wilson entered.

He stood for five minutes waiting to be recognized. Finally, The President looked up at Wilson. "Any good news, Will Thompson?"

"Yes and no. It's good that some of your critics were quiet for a change. But the total weight of the clippings is down by fifty percent. And actually, there were a few positive comments, one about one of your golf courses, 'The finest the man has ever played on,' and another recommending the spa in your New York s. . . s . . . s . . . skyscraper."

"That's all? Nothing good about my immigration policy or my hardline tariffs in the East?"

Wilson shook his head, "No, sir."

"That disappoints me. The weights have been low for two days now . . ."

"Five."

"Oh, yes, that's what I said, didn't I?"

After waiting for a response that never came, he added, "I'll have to pump out more tweets."

"But you've doubled the tweets every day since your first slow day."

"Oh, did I?" he asked, but quickly corrected himself, saying quietly, "Maybe it was just last night I did that." He whistled an unrecognizable tune and stared at the wall as Wilson stood with his arms crossed on his chest while waiting for him to talk.

Finally, The President verbalized, "The wife's going away tonight for the weekend. She's participating in some women's equal rights movement event in Syracuse. I'm invited, and I'm certain they'd want me to be there to thank me for how much I've done for their movement, more than any other president in history, but maybe my wife can do better at communicating with them about the issues they'll discuss. I suppose I'll just stay here and crank out a few tweets . . . but, I'm at a loss for words to say on Twitter. It seems like I've said everything about all I've done and all that needs to be done and all we could do if Congress would just work with me."

Wilson sensed a change in The President's mood, one he'd seen only rarely. He wasn't the proud, self confident, mow-them-all-down person he'd become accustomed to. *Is he depressed about his low approval ratings and the very low weights of the paper clippings?* he wondered. On an impulse, Wilson considered saying something he'd never been bold enough to ask before: *I'll invite myself to dine with The Man tonight.*

"How about I bring you a hamburger for dinner tonight, one of those monster burgers with onion rings and bacon? That'll get your mind flowing strong again. And I have a few ideas to float, if you are in the mood to listen."

The President looked up and nodded slowly. "The burger sounds good, but I want two of them, with a double order of French fries. And I don't know if I want to hear your ideas or not. There are just too many people who seem to think they know better than I how to run this country. I'll have burgers delivered to the West Gate at six. Pick them up and return here. Just come in. No need to knock since I'll know it's you."

Chapter 28

6 pm the same day. The Oval Office

Wilson carried the backpack from Mackril and the burgers that O'Donalds delivered.

The President was leaning back in his chair with his feet on the desk, clearly lost in thought, until he heard Wilson approaching. He abruptly sat erect, snatched a pen from the top drawer, and pretended to write on a paper on the desk.

Wilson opened the door without knocking, as he had been instructed to do. He approached the desk and waited for The President to take a break in his work. After several minutes, he was rewarded with a pleasant smile and a "Good to see you, Will Thompson."

The President rose quickly and moved a cushioned, gold, embroidered chair to the front of the desk. "Sit here," he said, as he took the dinner bag and placed it on the Resolute desk.

The President pressed the red button and sat looking at Wilson but remaining mute until the two Diet Cokes and condiments were brought in by a young man wearing black trousers and bow tie with a tuxedo shirt.

The President opened the paper wrap of one of the double-decker burgers and doused it with ketchup. Opening his mouth wide enough to munch through the entire thickness of an O'Double with bacon and extra cheese, he took a big bite and closed his eyes in enjoyment of his dinner.

Wilson bit through his burger a layer at a time. Halfway through his first, The President was already reaching in the bag for a second. One was enough for Wilson, and as he started on his large order of French fries, The President was finishing his second fries. The President sat with his elbows on the desk and his chin resting on his hands until Wilson finished eating. Then, he spoke quietly. "Will Thompson, let's talk politics."

Wilson no longer felt insecure being in presence of a world leader, or overwhelmed by extreme wealth and the many more years of The President's life experience. He had stood toe-to-toe with The President and contradicted him on occasions. *And The President listened.* That was a big-time confidence builder. He was well aware of his own lack of achievement, but today, that didn't matter. The most powerful people in the country clearly respected him. "Mr. President, my view of politics is limited by the numbers of articles I read. My opinions carry little weight because of my . . ."

"Enough of that, Will Thompson. I have many friends who possess all of what you think you lack. But I just don't trust them. Their advice centers primarily around their personal agendas, not mine. You are a tenderfoot, brand new to the DC scene, with no preconceived notions about government. You speak to me all the time about ideas that are current, not with the overtones of politics as you've witnessed in the past. You're a novice in this setting, just like me. Your mind is totally open, not closed like a steel trap to anyone's ideas except their own. I may seem overconfident to you, as I do to others. But that's just my . . . let's say 'protective shell'."

He paused in thought for a moment, then began talking in a quiet and serious tone.

"I'm going to share something with you, Wilson, that I've never told anyone before. I said 'tenderfoot' a moment ago. That refers to my one-time Boy Scout meeting when I was ten. I went, dressed in a tailor-made scout's uniform with a neat, red bandana around my neck. I felt so proud. For about ten seconds. Then, everyone attempted to humiliate me, asking questions about scout protocol from a manual that I'd never read before. I told them I didn't know what they were talking about. They laughed. At me. My starched, pressed, tailored uniform. My dropping a baseball the scout master tossed. They laughed. Though the term 'bullying' wasn't used back then, I was 'bullied'. And it hurt me. Deeply. I vowed never to tolerate another experience like that. And I never have, and certainly not since I became President. I stand toe-to-toe with people who try to dominate me. People ask me at times about issues in which I'm not fully versed. I refuse to say 'I don't know,' like I did at the scout meeting. I don't lie, like pundits say, but confabulate rather than be that boy scout again." The President turned away, wiped his eyes with the back of his hand, and cleared his throat before facing Wilson again.

"I suppose you feel insecure now, just like I did that one time in my life. I don't reveal myself to others as I have to you or take from others the little jabs you give me when I speak the facts improperly. You have corrected my factual accounts a number of times in our brief relationship. But the corrections were always given in a sensitive manner. You don't want to hurt my feelings; rather, your desire is to educate me as to the proper historical references so I look competent. I like that."

Wilson was surprised as much at the admission of The President's humiliation as he was with the intended compliment and being addressed by his proper name. This relaxed him to the extent that he welcomed the opportunity to speak when asked again. That was not long in coming.

"So Will Thompson, how will I do in the election in two years? Most national polls suggest the Democrats will win, but the same people that supported me in the last election pledge their complete support. Whom am I to believe?"

Wilson squirmed in his seat. *Here it goes. I must hold my cool and handle him like Mama said: Whip him up with the truth, then praise him to death.* But as he opened his mouth to speak, he knew this was the wrong approach. *The praise must come first.*

"There's no doubt that one hundred percent of your staunch supporters will be behind you again. You gave them exactly what they wanted. You quickly reduced taxes in a swift and powerful move."

The President smiled and leaned back in his chair.

Wilson felt even bolder as he realized that his stutter was now completely gone. He took a deep breath and continued. "You immediately tackled the immigration issue, just as you promised in your election campaign. You've encountered opposition, even within your own party, but you've kept plowing along. Even your opponents admire your tenacity in fighting Congress for the money you need. Though that's not yielded the result you want, you're picking up votes from the Independents, and even a few Democrats."

"Yes, I feel that myself. Go on."

"You receive considerable criticism on the issue of tariffs on trade with the Chinese."

The President frowned.

"But a solid group of Independents, as well as a few Democrats, are swaying in your favor, seeing that, despite initial losses, the long-term outlook is good for restoration of trade equality that will eventually happen and greatly boost our economy."

The President nodded. "Yes. I was astute in making that proclamation. I'll go down in history for my actions there."

He praised The President on several other issues before beginning the thrashing. He took a deep breath before making the transition. "Sir, you are a lot like President Rock Rollagin: He was an actor and you a hedge fund CEO. Both of you had no political experience at all."

The President smiled. "Yes, I am much like him, and even though he was extremely popular, I expect to exceed him as being one of the great presidents."

"He had forty percent of the electorate in his pocket within the first six months of his candidacy."

"Yes, exactly like I have now."

"But to be elected, he only had to add ten percent more voters to his list of supporters."

The President nodded. “Yes, you may be right about that.”

“So, you’re looking at just a small pickup in votes. Just ten percent, so where are the voters going to come from? The biggest attention is in the immigration issue.”

“Yes. I’ve taken a strong stand there. People like me for that.”

“But there’s a standoff with Congress in funding. You want five billion dollars to build a wall that will take four years to complete. It will take until 2022 for completion of The Great Wall, even if you started today.”

“Yes. I want that money now and I won’t back down.”

Wilson frowned and leaned toward The President. “And you’re too hardheaded to compromise!”

The President stood in a fury and threw the burger bag across the room. “I’ll never compromise!”

Wilson kept his composure as he continued, “Getting all the money is not a problem. Accept the two and a half billion they offer. That will allow construction of half The Great Wall of America by the time of the election in 2020. With the added seats you’ll gain in Congress in

2020 and The Great Wall that will be half-built, you can get the other two and a half billion as you start your second term in office and still have a completed The Great Wall of America by 2022."

The President seated himself and stared at Wilson.

"Throw in a few bones to Congress by giving them their immigration reform package."

"That will add billions to our national debt."

"No. The reform bill will streamline the immigration process and make the difficult and lengthy process of granting citizenship much faster. The costs per applicant will drop and lessen the payroll of the Department of Immigration. Take that savings and create a nicer environment for those waiting to be processed. Also, that act of goodwill will garner you a few of those voter percentage points you need for election."

"Humph. But I need *ten* percent."

"Then extract another five percent from the huge numbers of middle class voters. Give them some sort of tax break like you gave to the wealthy. That transition alone could put you over the top, not only by the Electoral College but also in the popular vote."

The President shook his head. “No.”

By this time, Wilson felt emboldened to get to the papa mode of his ma/pa approach. He took a deep breath, then leaned toward The Man. “You know something, sir, you’re so smart about stock and bond investments but totally dumb about people.”

The President stood and glared.

“And the tariffs you placed on imports. For certain, you’re thinking about the long-term profits, but you’re dealing with countries that don’t have an election coming up in two years. They may *never* have an election, while you are gambling on quick treaties with nations that can toy with you for a long time. Decades even. Swallow your pride and resolve the tariff issue now. Don’t let our farmers and merchants suffer. You had the farm vote in the last election. Of your sixty million votes, three million of them were farmers who voted for you. If they are still suffering on the next election, they’ll kiss you goodbye. That’s three million votes you’ll have to make up elsewhere.”

“You’re no help. Why did I ever confide in you?”

Wilson stood, placed both hands on the Resolute desk, and knitted his brow. "Because you need me. Someone to give you a reality check." He looked away for a second before continuing in a soft voice. "You may never be here in 2020, with all the people who want to assassinate you. You may be dead and gone by then."

"What?! What are you talking about?"

"About your deceased secretary of defense, Dapper, whom you jabbed with a drug with which he was trying to kill you. Danny Dapper, your own cabinet appointee! Who helped him plan his attack? Four others, all your own cabinet members! And how about the five senators who are in the hospital still sick from the scorpion fish poison they'd planned to use on you? Four were Democrats but one was a Republican. Republican? That's your party, if you've forgotten." He paused to take a breath.

"In another group trying to poison you, four Democrats worked with a Republican. Senator Wilting. The Strictnun that nearly killed him was meant for you. And Jonas Hopalong? A Republican now deceased from homemade benzodiazepine? Rumor has it the drug was meant for you. So, you ask for bipartisanship? There you have it. Republicans and Democrats who agree on one thing, to get rid of YOU!" He pointed at The President.

"You knew all this and didn't report it to the FBI?!" yelled The President. "I'll have you and all these others thrown in jail for treason!"

Wilson shook his head. "Why would you want to do that? You gained several percentages of the votes you need by your attempted resuscitation of Secretary Dapper. The senators with fish poison and Strictnun were avid supporters of you before you stopped listening to and working with them, and to learn that they wanted you dead will wipe out votes from all their supporters. And me? In prison? There are tens of millions of people in my lower class that will side with my story when the press covers it. Subtract all that from the votes needed for your re-election? Mr. President, you're coming up a few votes short of being elected, and the Electoral College won't be there to save you this time."

The President pursed his lips and stared at Wilson. In a calm voice he stated, "I feel that you're not finished with your lashing of me. Give me the rest of your message."

Wilson took the briefcase and opened it on The President's desk. "Here's another drug some of your 'faithful Republicans' want me to use on you."

"They wanted *you* to kill *me*?"

"No. They want you alive — but as a cooperative President who will listen to a little advice when it's given."

The President leaned over and looked in the box. "Ok. Tell me what this is all about."

"The drug one of your so-called 'loyal followers' wants to give you is Jimson weed. Given as they instructed, it will temporarily subdue parts of your brain to make you temporarily cooperative."

"Like a Zombie?"

"Exactly. They want me to give you a measured portion of Jimson weed to have you subdued to the point of what they term 'rational behavior' . . ."

"Do my own Republican supporters think I'm not always rational?"

"You said that, not me. But I have a proposal for you. I'll take the Jimson weed myself, as they directed that I give to you. You can see how it affects me. That will prove to you that murder was not their intention."

"That's ok, so far."

"Next, you can try it yourself . . ."

"No, not me. I don't eat stuff that can alter any of my body functions."

"Or, we'll call an emergency meeting of Congress. Tonight. What I'm proposing now is a setup by some people in your White House. They're waiting for your invite to them and congressional leaders to a get-together. Tonight. Gather them here, and pretend to be under the influence of the drug . . ."

"I'm a good actor. Let me think about that."

"And discuss one of the bills they're not being helpful with . . ."

"That'll be The Great Wall of America. The one to stop all the illegals from entering America. That's my priority. But I need all five billion."

"You are well aware of the fact that if you have all five billion dollars, the wall wouldn't be complete until 2022?"

"Yes. 2022 is the projected completion date."

"Think about accepting two installments of that money, two and a half now, which will build half the wall in 2020, and two and a half billion after you're re-elected in 2020, which will complete the entire wall in 2022. And you know you're going to get the votes then; more Republicans will be elected to the House, and the Senate will still have a Republican majority. Today, everyone will accept your offer of a meeting with some hope of reconciling your differences. They fully expect I'll give you the weed and that you'll mellow to the extent you'll make compromises. Just as you should have already done."

"But they know how strongly I feel about The Great Wall of America, and I will never be that little boy scout again, Will Thompson."

"If you want to win, you need to do something to earn those votes. After you see the effect of the Jimson weed on me, maybe you could take just a pinch of it and relax yourself a little. It's not a drug like the tranquilizers doctors prescribe. It's a plant that grows organically, with no fertilizers or hormones added, and it's as common as any other plant that grows in this area. There are no concealed poisons, and so long as you don't gulp it down in double doses like you do your hamburgers, it's perfectly safe."

The President's serious look turned neutral and then to a smile before he laughed. "I take it that you regard me as being piggish in the way I devour my O'Doubles and fries."

Wilson began to smile himself as he saw a changed Mr. President.

The President sat at his desk, leaning back, with his face in his hands. "Give me a few minutes to think about all this," he said, as he pressed the red button.

While The President thought, Wilson measured out the dosage of Jimson weed the letter prescribed and washed it down with a fresh, cold Diet Coke.

The drug took effect within two minutes. Initially, there was a warmth that engulfed his body. Then, a feeling of euphoria was followed by thirst. He emptied his can of Coke, walked around the Resolute desk, and pressed the red button. He never saw the service man bring it in, but almost immediately, there was another Diet Coke in front of him. His pupillary dilatation caused a light sensitivity, making him squint. He was aware of the presence of his President, which made him sit erect and await direction.

"You took the Jimson weed a half hour ago, and you're real quiet. How do you feel, Will Thompson?" were words he heard loud and clear.

"I feel great, sir. It's such a pleasure to be here in your office."

"Do you experience any pain?"

"No, sir. I feel good and at peace with the world."

"Do you recall why you came to my office to-day?"

"Oh, yes, sir. Your friends sent me here because they want so much for you to succeed."

The President explored the drug reaction still fur-ther with the question, "Why did they send you here with that poison, to kill me?"

"That never happened. These senators and cabinet members know that your success ensures their jobs. That sounds selfish on their part, but they really worship you."

The President smiled and pumped out his chest.

"What about the others that made attempts on my life?"

"Half are staunch Republicans who think you're going to lose this election, all because you won't compromise on any issue. They think you're establishing a dictatorship. The others are Democrats that want the country to move ahead on issues that are stagnant. They don't want their years in Congress wasted when there is so much to be done."

The President frowned and screamed, "Tell me the names of all the individuals that are with you in this evil plot!"

Wilson smiled as he stood to face The President. "They shall remain anonymous, so I will take all the blame. The drug makes me feel so happy; I want to spill my heart out to you. You are a good President, not a great one as yet, but you can be if you listen to well-given advice and stop snapping off directorial tweets without fully listening to your advisers. Unless you change your style, you will also lose enough of the Republican five Senate seats in the 2020 election to shift the majority to the Democrats. Maybe your loyal followers will be enough to gain the election yourself, but without a Senate majority, you will be that boy scout again, with no chance to have your way on anything. The country wants a strong man, like you, but it abhors the thought of having a dictator. And I do as well." Wilson reached over the desk and took The President's cell phone. "Let's not use Twitter for just two days. A lot of people resent what you're doing with that medium."

The President looked at Wilson, too stunned to even speak.

Wilson felt weird. The drug made him totally carefree in his honest answer of the question, which he never would have fully felt without it. But he felt good about what he said and had no regrets. If he was fired, so be it. He'd kicked The President's butt and was proud of it.

Chapter 29

10 pm the same night. The Cabinet Room

The next hour after taking the Jimson weed had been fuzzy. Wilson was totally aware of things that were happening, but he had no control.

Then he was in a chair against the wall in the Cabinet Room, which was packed with cabinet members and congressmen sitting at the table and in several rows of chairs circling it. The President listened more than he spoke as business was conducted. He saw The President stagger a few times as he walked in the room. Wilson was in a fog but was aware of every word that was spoken. What was that unusual alteration of The President's diction? Was he pretending to have ingested Jimson weed? Or was he on the Zombie drug as well? Life was a dream as he saw the Speaker of the House, the Senate minority leader, party Whips, the committee chairs, the . . . He nodded off to sleep but was aroused by Hollie Mackril giving him a hug. A man in a black suit with a tuxedo shirt walked by carrying a tray of hors d'oeuvres. Hollie lifted two, popping one in her mouth and placing one on his lips. Wilson was hungry, downing that and accepting a second that Hollie offered.

He heard someone shout, "Holy Mackril, I'm glad to see you here."

He had a vague memory that she slapped the man with a glove and said, "It's 'Hollie'."

Wilson looked for The President but never saw him as the room filled with people and food and spinning chandeliers, the twirling kaleidoscope of colors, and a table with food on it suspended on a side wall. Congresspeople walked on the ceiling above his head, and from somewhere, the sound of the National Anthem played softly in his head. The President, who had a lampshade on his head, danced with Hollie, and the lady Speaker of the House with the Republican minority leader . . . as chairs moved through the air . . . and stars shined through the ceiling . . . and there were visions of laughter and handshaking and back slapping . . . He tried to get up — he felt like dancing — dreams were so beautiful he wanted to . . .

Chapter 30

8 am the next morning. The Oval Office

Wilson awakened in the morning with a start. He looked around and saw that he was in The President's office, lying on a sofa that was not a part of the office yesterday. The President was there reading at his desk.

Wilson sat up and rubbed his eyes. "Where are all the people that were here last night?"

"I dunno. I hope Congress is in session today, but no one has told me that."

A President who was so warm and open to Wilson last night was coldly indifferent, like someone else.

"Well, tell me. What happened last night when I was tanked on the Jimson weed?"

"I dunno. I had a pinch of it myself and did something totally idiotic."

"Huh?"

"I listened to a neophyte like you. I've never taken a drug in my life. Now my entire future is up in the air."

"Tell me about it."

His words were ignored.

After a few moments of silence, The President spoke. "It's time for you to go home."

Wilson waited for some sort of explanation, but two security guards came and grabbed his arms, leading him to the door.

"I'll bring the weighed newspaper clippings to you tomorrow."

"No. That won't be necessary."

'Well, am I to come back here next week?"

The President never looked up as he said, "No. You're fired."

Wilson was led out the door without any further explanation. The silent guards drove him to his garage apartment and let him out.

Wilson had recovered from the night's Jimson weed and felt like himself, except for a sense of regret that he'd done something so stupid as being extremely critical of a man so wildly in need of praise and reassurance. The preposterous idea of proposing the Zombie drug was a thing only an idiot would say to any person, let alone The President. *What was I thinking? What a fool to believe I could help make a difference and save The President and the country.*

It was a long weekend for Wilson, with two days to ponder how he could take care of his family. It was his own fault. His irrational action had cost him his job, or perhaps even his loss of liberty if The President chose to prosecute him for not reporting his knowledge of the attempted assassinations and his role in administering the Zombie drug.

Wilson had always been a happy person who bounced back quickly after setbacks in life. He tried to sleep off his state of depression but could not get comfortable. As he lay down on the sofa, there was a painful pressure under his belt. He tossed and turned a few minutes, but he had a strange feeling. Something was in stuck in his pocket. He twisted and turned it until he could pull it out. It was The President's cell phone.

It was a weekend of regret for Wilson. On Sunday night, he received a call to come to the White House at 5:30 am the next day to gather his things.

Chapter 31

5:30 am Monday. The Oval Office

Wilson opened the door and saw that a stack of newspapers and magazines cluttered the Resolute desk. The President was busy with a large pair of scissors, clipping articles. Wilson walked to the desk and stood with his hands clasped on his waist, waiting for his verdict.

The President weighed the last of the articles before looking up. "You weren't here to do your job, so I did it for you."

Wilson did not retaliate with a defensive rebuttal. "Yes, sir," was his only answer.

"I didn't have my cell phone, so I never had the opportunity to tweet anything."

"I'm sorry about that, sir." He reached in his pocket, withdrew The President's iPhone, and placed it on his desk.

"The weight of Saturday's articles about me was as low as they'd been the last week."

A quiet "Yes, sir," was again the only response Wilson could muster.

"Sunday's weight was way up. It was one of the biggest days since I started recording this data."

Wilson nodded.

"There was something unusual about the reports about me."

"Yes, sir."

"Ninety percent of the articles praised my actions. I read them all."

Wilson looked up. "That's good, isn't it?"

"Yes, it is. And you know the reason I had you clip and weigh the articles about me?"

"Tell me."

"It was because everything written about me pointed to me as a bad guy. I got to the point of not reading *any* of them. The weights you gave me were the only records I kept after I made up the idea about bad news being as positive as the good. Yes, there was little good news, so I had stopped reading and began weighing the good and bad, like we talked about when you started your job here."

"So, can I get my job back?"

"No. There is no job for you to even have back, as long as the positivity continues. I want to read the reports that praise me. I just devour them all."

"Wait! I've been out of touch this weekend. What happened Friday night that had made you so upset?"

"I made the mistake of following somebody's advice. Yours. I acted sorta like I was drugged: After I saw how good you felt, and yet how clearly you spoke and acted while on it, I took a pinch of the Jimson weed, and that added to the illusion. And then I negotiated, with the idea of taking the two and a half billion. They were reticent. Then I did the unthinkable. I called in the kitchen staff and had them make finger foods. I went to the kitchen and personally added a sprinkling of your Jimson weed. I actually tasted it. It was good. I had the wine steward uncork six of the best bottles of champagne usually reserved for guests of state, the Krug Close the Messy Deal, at a thousand dollars a bottle. As strongly as I wanted to experience the taste and texture of that fine wine, my compulsion against alcohol ingestion prevented my tasting it. But the others did and followed with the hors d'oeuvres.

In the middle of The President's explanation, a young attendant entered silently. He wore tuxedo pants, a bow tie, and a tuxedo shirt with fancy ruffles down the front. He walked to a corner table and positioned the lampshade he carried onto a shadeless lamp.

The President's eyes batted toward the young man and back to Wilson. "Maybe I was a little high myself, as I never saw them as even a little stoned. But when I brought up my Great Wall of America again, they came to an agreement right away."

"Did you ask for the entire five billion?"

"I probably could have, but your idea of halving that seemed logical, at least it seemed so at that time."

"Did you throw in the Immigration Reform Package?"

"Will Thompson, I could have asked them for a hundred billion, and they would have agreed. But that wasn't right. I had an advantage, and it just seemed fair to *give* them the reform bill, even though they never asked about it. I had the notion that *they were the Zombies*, not me."

Wilson looked up to see The President wearing a big smile. The President was on one of his long-waits-between-words jags, so Wilson stood patiently.

"The pundits ate that up, Republicans and Democrats alike. They're writing it up as if I'm a changed man, especially since I didn't tweet anything. On Sunday morning TV, two members of my cabinet who'd been cool in our relationship the past few months called me the greatest President of the century. I liked that. Tiger Schweitzer gave a special program with Democrats, and they were excited about working with the 'New' President. They promised they'd work with my White House and immediately craft legislation to resolve The Great Wall of America issue as well as Immigration Reform."

"Congratulations."

"I'm giving you a little of the credit for the transition, for agreeing with my plan to make the compromises I proposed. I'm not certain if the tiny bit of the drug you gave me helped or not, but it did make me a little euphoric and boosted my confidence."

After a long period of silence, Wilson said, “That’s just great, sir. I’ll grab my things and leave now. So, I guess this is goodbye. I’ve enjoyed working with you. I’ll return to my maintenance job on Capitol Hill.”

“No. You’ve been replaced there as well.”

Wilson’s heart sank. *If I’m blacklisted, how will I ever find work and be able to support my family?* He started to speak but choked up. He turned to exit.

“But wait. I’ve created a position for you here in the White House.”

Wilson looked up through moistened eyes.

“And there’s a fifty thousand dollar raise. You’ll be my Library Director, to give me writings you think I’ll enjoy. And . . . and . . .”

Wilson leaned forward for his words.

“Maybe we can work together on another legislative compromise. What are your ideas on keeping the farmers’ vote?”

~ THE END ~

Acknowledgements

Thanks to Richard Krevolin for his genius in storytelling. His late night phone calls (he's on PDT and I'm on EDT) and corrective emails kept me wide-eyed and working far past my 9-to-5 standard workday. Believe me, I felt battered and bruised after some of those roughhouse sessions. But the product speaks for his demanding tactics, for this book as well as those of my future publications.

Nancy Cohen is also a slave driver. She makes certain the 101 dalmations are not 99 or 105. Her demand of exactness in detail is much more precise than given me by my surgical mentors at Vanderbilt and Duke. Her sense of humor surprised me. For one with such rigid attention to even the most minor of details, she made some great suggestions that enhanced the humor. I like what she added to the book.

Yes, I like Ana Magno's work on the final version of the cover, but her value to this book was even far greater than drawing out the cover and stenciling words. She offered recommendations that are reflected in the text and in the book's definitive titling. Thanks, Ana.

My appreciation to John Haslett for his continued support.

And as always, I'm grateful to my sons. Barclay is the best fisherman in the family. He can recognize when I'm in the funk of a "writer's block" and always revives me with a fishing trip in the Chesapeake Bay. Glenn Jr., an anthropologist, is the best writer in the family. His descriptions of Amazonian shamans, uncontacted indigenous tribes, jaguars on the prowl, Machiguenga and Kayapo Indians, and medicinal plants are photographic reality. I wish I could do that . . .

~

Made in the USA
San Bernardino, CA
11 November 2019

59706737R10129